365
Stories and Rhymes for Boys

Illustrated by Andy Everitt-Stewart, Ruth Galloway, Martin Remphry and Jan Smith.

Additional illustrations by John Bendall Brunello, Bill Bolton, Andy Catling, Caroline Jayne Church, Jacqueline East, Frank Endersby, Daniel Howarth, Steve Smallman, Kristina Stephenson and Claire Tindall.

Written by Cecil Frances Alexander, Tina Barrett, Janet Allison Brown, Lewis Carroll, Charles F. Carryl, Kate Cary, Deborah Chancellor, Andy Charman, Arthur Hugh Clough, Geoff Cowan, Meryl Doney, Nick Ellsworth, Gaby Goldsack, Kenneth Grahame, Jillian Harker, Ann Harth, Heather Henning, James Hogg, Liz Holliday, Janey Joseph, Claire Keene, Karen King, Rudyard Kipling, Alison Milford, Jan Payne, Beatrice Phillpotts, Ronne Randall, Willam Brighty Rands, Caroline Repchuck, Christina Rossetti, Kath Smith, Louisa Somerville, Robert Louis Stevenson, Christine Tagg, Edward Thomas, Gordon Volke, Candy Wallace, Maureen Warner and Kat Wootton.

Every effort has been made to acknowledge the contributors to this book. If we have made any errors, we will be pleased to rectify them in future editions.

This edition published by Parragon Books Ltd in 2013

Parragon Books Ltd
Chartist House
15-17 Trim Street
Bath BA1 1HA, UK
www.parragon.com

ISBN 978-1-4723-3671-2

Printed in China

365
Stories and Rhymes
for Boys

PaRragon
Bath · New York · Singapore · Hong Kong · Cologne · Delhi
Melbourne · Amsterdam · Johannesburg · Shenzhen

Contents

Contents

Contents

Contents

Shadow's Lucky Charm

Dark shadows of evening hung over the television studios. Bustling by day, now the place stood empty. Only Sam, the security officer, remained. His torch shone as he made his rounds, checking everything was shut down.

As he stepped into Studio One, Sam shivered. Why was it always so cold in there? Sam didn't wait to find out. He felt he was being watched.

No sooner had he gone, than...

"Lights, cameras, action!" called Click, a ghostly producer. A creepy cast began to play their parts in the spooky soap opera, *Haunted House*, followed feverishly by ghosts everywhere.

"I can't pretend to be a scary phantom," hissed Grey Ghost to Camera Two.

"I haven't got the spirit for it!"

"Well, don't tell anybody!" smiled Shadow, delivering her lines in the lead role. "It'll be our secret. Besides..."

Suddenly, she froze.

"What's wrong?" asked Grey Ghost.

"I'm going to have to leave the show," said Shadow, unhappily. "I've lost my lucky wishbone. I can't go on without it – I get terrible stage fright."

So *Haunted House* didn't transmit that night.

Early next evening, the sweetest phantom cat Shadow had ever seen stepped through the wall of the studio.

"Who are you?" asked Shadow, curiously.

"I'm Lucky," purred the cat. "I move as silently as a shadow."

"Shadow is my name!" laughed Shadow.

"I've always wanted to be in a TV show," mewed Lucky.

"I want to be out of one," replied Shadow, sadly explaining.

Lucky looked thoughtful. "I've just had a *purrrfect* idea," he said, whispering into Shadow's ear.

Shadow let out a spine-chilling shriek of joy.

"Shadow, are you all right?" asked Grey Ghost.

"I am now," smiled Shadow.

"Lights, cameras, action!" called Click, when filming on *Haunted House* began the next night.

This time, there was an extra ghost in the high-spirited cast. Lucky was delighted with his glide-on part, and Shadow was even happier about it – her faultless performance proved it. After all, she had a new Lucky charm.

And as for any stage fright, there simply wasn't a ghost of a chance it would return now!

Witch's Brew

Eye of lizard, toe of frog,
Tail of rat and bark of dog.
Sneeze of chicken, cough of bat,
Lick of weasel, smell of cat.
Stir it up and mix it well,
To make a magic monster spell.

Now it's done, the spell is ready,
The monster's rising, slow and steady.
"Pleased to meet you," Winnie sighs.
"Pleased to eat you," he replies.
What's gone wrong, she cannot tell,
To spoil the magic monster spell.

The witch goes pale, she must act fast,
Or else this day may be her last!
She grabs her wand. She has a notion
Of how to get rid of this potion.
She shakes her wand, which breaks the spell,
And waves the monster fond farewell!

A Spelling Lesson

Wanda Witch went wandering,
Within a spooky wood.
She loved to practise spooky spells,
And hated being good!

She crept up on a wizard,
And before he could respond,
Wanda waved her wand and he
Fell straight into a pond!

Although it was not very deep,
The wizard soon saw red.
He cast a spell which made his cloak
Flap right round Wanda's head.

It wrapped around her body,
And squeezed her really tight.
"Say sorry," roared the wizard,
"Or stay like that all night!"

The witch agreed and told him,
"Your magic is so fast.
No more naughty spells from me,
I've really cast my last!"

Fee, Fi, Fo, Fum!

Fee, fi, fo, fum,
I smell the blood
Of an Englishman:
Be he alive or be he dead,
I'll grind his bones
To make my bread.

Little Hare

Round about there
Sat a little hare,
The bow-wows came and chased him
Right up there!

Ten O'Clock Scholar

A diller, a dollar,
A ten o'clock scholar,
What makes you come so soon?
You used to come at ten o'clock,
But now you come at noon.

Round About

Round about the rose bush,
Three steps,
Four steps,
All the little boys and girls
Are sitting
On the doorsteps.

The Magpie

Magpie, magpie, flutter and flee,
Turn up your tail and good luck come to me.

John Smith

Is John Smith within?
Yes, that he is.
Can he set a shoe?
Aye, marry, two;
Here a nail and there a nail,
Tick, tack, too.

I Wish...

I wish I was an elephant,
'Cause it would make me laugh.
To use my nose like a garden hose
To rinse myself in the bath.

I wish I was a chameleon,
Chameleons are best.
I'd change my colour and life would be fuller,
For a change is as good as a rest.

I wish I was a dolphin,
A dolphin would be my wish.
Leaping and splashing, I'd be very dashing,
And swim along with the fish.

I wish I was an ostrich,
An ostrich would be grand.
But if I got scared, would I be prepared
To bury my head in the sand?

I wish I had more wishes,
But now my game is through,
I'm happy to be quite simply me,
Enjoying a day at the zoo.

The Dotty Professor

Professor Von Bean was very excited. He had finished building his machine and it was ready to use. It was the most complicated contraption he had ever built.

The professor called his assistant to come to watch him start the machine. The wheels were green and brown, and there were levers on either side. The side panels were striped red and white, and there was a big chimney on the top for the smoke to escape. There was a cupboard on the side which, the professor explained, was to hang a wet coat in. There was a shelf on the back for a box of plants.

While Professor Von Bean was getting more and more excited, his assistant looked very worried.

"But what does it do?" he asked, timidly.

The professor scratched his head and thought.

"Oh dear, oh dear!" he sighed. "What a fool I have been! Why didn't I think of that? It does absolutely nothing useful at all!"

The Cow

The friendly cow all red and white,
I love with all my heart:
She gives me cream with all her might,
To eat with apple-tart.

She wanders lowing here and there,
And yet she cannot stray,
All in the pleasant open air,
The pleasant light of day.

And blown by all the winds that pass
And wet with all the showers,
She walks among the meadow grass
And eats the meadow flowers.

The Fieldmouse

Where the acorn tumbles down,
Where the ash tree sheds its berry,
With your fur so soft and brown,
With your eye so round and merry,
Scarcely moving the long grass,
Fieldmouse, I can see you pass.

Fieldmouse, fieldmouse, do not go,
Where the farmer stacks his treasure,
Find the nut that falls below,
Eat the acorn at your pleasure,
But you must not steal the grain
He has stacked with so much pain.

Make your hole where mosses spring,
Underneath the tall oak's shadow,
Pretty, quiet, harmless thing,
Play about the sunny meadow.
Keep away from corn and house,
None will harm you, little mouse.

Tractor Trouble

Farmer Fred sped off on his tractor to his first job of the day.
"Woof! Woof!" barked Patch as the tractor whizzed past at
high speed. The tractor was going too fast!
In the next field, Harry Horse trotted
over to see what the noise was about.
He stuck his head over the hedge
just as the tractor rushed past.
"Yuck!" neighed Harry, as he
was splattered with lumps of
sticky mud.
But Farmer Fred didn't hear.
He was already on his way to his
next job – collecting bales of hay to feed the cows with.
In no time at all, Farmer Fred had hitched up the trailer of
hay to the tractor.
"We'll have those cows fed before you can say dandelions,"
smiled Farmer Fred.
Farmer Fred rushed across Cowslip Meadow. The hay bales
bounced this way and that. Patch raced after them.
"Woof! Woof!" barked Patch. The hay bales didn't look
safe. But it was too late. A hay bale bounced off the trailer
towards Connie Cow.
"Moo!" cried poor Connie as she jumped into the brook to
avoid a tumbling bale of hay.
"We've finished all our jobs in record time!" said Farmer

Fred as he arrived in the farmyard. "Now, where is everyone?"

Farmer Fred looked around the yard, but he couldn't see any of the animals.

Just then, Patch came running into the yard. "Woof! Woof!" he barked.

"What is it, Patch?" asked Farmer Fred, puzzled. "Do you know where everyone has gone?"

Farmer Fred followed Patch out of the yard. Harry Horse, Polly Pig, Shirley Sheep and Hetty Hen were standing beside the brook.

Farmer Fred couldn't believe his eyes when he saw Connie Cow stuck in the brook.

"Blithering beetroots!" Farmer Fred gasped. "How did you get in there?"

"Moo!" said Connie Cow crossly.

"Never fear," said Farmer Fred cheerfully, as he disappeared into the barn. "I've an idea!"

"I hope poor Connie is rescued soon," said Polly Pig. "You know how her milk curdles when she's upset!"

Just then, the door to the shed flew open and out came Farmer Fred, dragging...

"...The Inflatable Cow-floater," said Farmer Fred proudly. And off he bumped towards the brook.

Harry Horse and the others followed at a safe distance.

Within minutes, Farmer Fred had launched his Inflatable Cow-floater and was busy telling Connie Cow to climb aboard.

The animals held their breath as Connie Cow wibbled and wobbled on top of the Inflatable Cow-floater.

Then there was a scraping sound and a loud hiss.

Connie Cow and the Inflatable Cow-floater sank back into the water.

"Patch," clucked Hetty Hen. "We have to rescue poor Connie."

"I'd pull her out myself, but," sighed Harry Horse, "I'm not as young as I was."

"The tractor is the only one who can help her now," Polly Pig grunted.

"Woof, woof!" barked Patch, picking up the rope attached to the back of the tractor.

"That's it! I've an even better idea!" shouted Farmer Fred. "I know just how to rescue Connie."

Farmer Fred drove the

tractor down to the edge of the brook. He tied the rope to the Cow-floater.

"Poor Connie," mumbled Harry Horse, shaking his mud-splattered head.

Slowly and carefully, Farmer Fred pulled the Cow-floater out of the brook. At last, Connie Cow was safe on dry land. All the animals cheered.

Later, in the farmyard, Farmer Fred was feeling very pleased with himself.

"Look!" he said, showing Jenny the list all ticked off, "I've finished all the jobs... and thanks to the tractor, I've had time to rescue Connie!"

Jenny looked at Patch and smiled.

Tom, He Was a Piper's Son

Tom, he was a piper's son,
He learnt to play when he was young,
And the only tune that he could play,
Was, 'Over the hills and far away'.
Over the hills and a great way off,
The wind shall blow my topknot off!

The Squirrel

The winds they did blow,
The leaves they did wag;
Along came a beggar boy,
And put me in his bag.

He took me to London,
A lady me did buy,
Put me in a silver cage,
And hung me up on high.

With apples by the fire,
And nuts for me to crack,
Besides a little feather bed
To rest my little back.

Go to Bed, Tom

Go to bed, Tom, go to bed, Tom,
Tired or not, Tom, go to bed, Tom.

Round and Round the Garden

Round and round the garden,
Like a teddy bear.
One step, two steps,
Tickly under there!

Charley Warley

Charley Warley had a cow,
Black and white about the brow;
Open the gate and let her through,
Charley Warley's old cow.

Daddy

Bring Daddy home with a fiddle and a drum,
A pocket full of spices, an apple and a plum.

Monster Marathon

"Very nice," said Cyril the Cyclops, eyeing his reflection in a puddle. He was wearing running shoes, running shorts and a running vest. Cyril the Cyclops had entered the annual Monster Marathon, and he had his eye on the trophy.

On the other side of Monster Mountain, two mischievous goblins were busy planning their own strategy for the big race. Bogey and Burp were identical twin brothers, and only their mother could tell them apart.

"So," Bogey was saying, "we'll swap at the crooked tree."

"That's the plan," agreed Burp.

The day of the Monster Marathon dawned. A large banner saying **ANNUAL MONSTER MARATHON** fluttered in the breeze, and the field was steadily filling up with all manner of monsters. Cyril watched as a troop of trolls jogged by wearing matching tracksuits with Team Troll neatly embroidered on the back, looking very professional. He suddenly felt nervous.

The stout monster official raised the starting pistol into the still air. There was a deafening hush followed by a pistol shot, and the monsters were off!

Cyril did his best, but as he approached the halfway mark he could go no further. It was no good, he had to rest. He slumped down by the side of a crooked tree and almost immediately nodded off – but only moments later he was disturbed by voices.

"It's OK, he's fast asleep," someone said. Cyril kept very still and opened his eye just enough to see the goblin twins swapping clothes and Bogey sprinting off into the distance.

Cyril knew what was going on. He had to get to the monster official and tell him what he had seen before it was too late. As soon as Burp had gone too, he jumped up and ran as fast as his

tired legs could carry him. He reached the finish line just in time to see the trophy being presented to a grinning Bogey.

"*Stop!*" shrieked Cyril. "They're cheats!"

In a breathless voice Cyril explained what had happened.

"Nonsense," complained Burp, "I'm his coach. My brother won fair and square."

The monster official gazed from one goblin to the other.

"Then why," he said slowly, pointing to Burp's T-shirt, "are your clothes on inside out?"

And although Cyril hadn't won the race, he was awarded an extra-special trophy for his vigilance and sense of fair play.

Tractor's Busy Day

Here's the tractor, shiny and new.
Chug chug chug! There's so much to do.

The tractor starts a busy day,
Delivering sacks of bales and hay.

Bumpety-bump! The ground is rough,
But the tractor's wheels are wide and tough.

Slow and careful, big and strong,
The tractor tows the trailer along.

The tractor crosses up and down,
Ploughing the field, all muddy and brown.

Well done, Tractor! Chug chug chug!
Now home to the barn where it's warm and snug.

Tugboat

The tugboat blows his horn to say,
Toot! Toot! Toot! Please make way!

Little Tugboat's tough and strong,
He's built to tow big ships along.

Pushing, pulling! Tug! Tug! Tug!
Backwards, forwards! Chug! Chug! Chug!

Tugboat guides a ship to shore,
Then off he goes to help some more.

Tugboat never gets out of puff,
Even when the waves are rough!

Rain or sunshine, wind or fog –
Toot! Toot! Tugboat loves his job!

Bone Crazy

Alfie sat in his basket chewing on a large bone. Mmm! It tasted good.

When he had chewed it for long enough, he took it down to the bottom of the garden, to bury it in his favourite spot beneath the old oak tree. He didn't see next door's dog, Ferdy, watching him through a hole in the fence.

The next day, when Alfie went to dig up his bone, it was gone! He dug all around, but it was nowhere to be found. Then he spied a trail of muddy paw prints leading to the fence, and he guessed what had happened.

Alfie was too big to fit through the fence and get his bone back, so he thought of a plan, instead. Next day he buried another bone. This time, he knew Ferdy was watching him.

Later Alfie hid and watched as Ferdy crept into the garden and started to dig up the bone. Suddenly, Ferdy yelped in pain. The bone had bitten his nose! He flew across the garden and through the fence, leaving the bone behind.

Alfie's friend Mole crept out from where the bone was buried. How the two friends laughed at their trick! And from then on, Ferdy always kept safely to his side of the fence.

One Stormy Night

It was Patch's first night outside in his smart new kennel. He snuggled down on his blanket and watched as dusk fell.

Before long he fell fast asleep. As he slept, big spots of rain began to fall. A splash of water dripped from the kennel roof onto his nose.

Then there was a great crash and a bright flash of light lit up the sky.

Patch woke with a start and was on his feet at once, growling and snarling. "Just a silly storm," he told himself. "Nothing to scare a farm dog!"

But as the lightning flashed yet again, he saw a great shadow looming against the barn. Patch gulped. Whatever could it be? He began to bark furiously, trying to act braver than he felt – and sure enough, next time the lightning flashed, there was no sign of the shadow. "I soon scared that monster away!" he thought.

But as Patch settled back down, the sky outside lit up once more. There in the doorway towered the monster!

"Just checking you're okay in the storm," said Mummy.

"A fearless farm dog like me?" said Patch. "Of course I am!" But as the storm raged on, he snuggled up close to her all the same!

The Lost Rocket

Zack stared out of the window at Mum's brand-new space rocket.

It had blue and silver stripes and shone in the starlight.

Zack really wanted to fly it. But he knew Mum wouldn't let him.

Mum put on her space helmet. "I'm off to the space station now, Zack," she said. "Be good."

She stepped into the teleporter, and disappeared into thin air.

Zack looked at the space rocket. "I could fly that rocket now," he said to himself. "I bet it's really easy." He put on his space suit, went out to the rocket and slid open the door.

Mum had left the starter crystal in the ignition pad.

Once the door was safely closed, Zack took off his helmet and pushed down the crystal. The rocket's

engines fired up. Zack gulped. It was now or never.

"I'll be back by lunch time," he thought.

At first everything seemed easy. Zack made it safely past planet Earth, and began to head for Mars. But then a comet came rushing towards Zack. He grabbed the controls, but he couldn't make the rocket swerve away quickly enough. He was going to crash!

"What on earth are you doing, you naughty boy?"

It was Mum! She was right next to Zack.

She grabbed the controls and the rocket swerved away from the comet. It was just in time. "I picked up your SOS, and teleported myself here double-quick," Mum said.

Mum looked at Zack. "Just wait till I get you home!" she said with an angry frown. Zack had a feeling that he might be grounded for a very long time. But for once, he didn't mind too much!

Two Little Dicky Birds

Two little dicky birds sitting on a wall,
One named Peter, one named Paul.
Fly away, Peter!
Fly away, Paul!
Come back, Peter!
Come back, Paul!

Once I Saw a Little Bird

Once I saw a little bird
Come hop, hop, hop,
So I cried, "Little bird,
Will you stop, stop, stop?"
And was going to the window,
To say, "How do you do?"
But he shook his little tail,
And far away he flew.

Little Robin Redbreast

Little Robin Redbreast
Sat upon a rail:
Niddle-noddle went his head!
Wiggle-waggle went his tail.

Intery, Mintery, Cutery, Corn

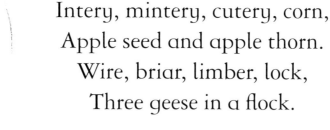

Intery, mintery, cutery, corn,
Apple seed and apple thorn.
Wire, briar, limber, lock,
Three geese in a flock.

One flew east and one flew west;
One flew over the cuckoo's nest.

The North Wind Doth Blow

The north wind doth blow,
And we shall have snow,
And what will poor Robin do then?
Poor thing!

He'll sit in a barn,
And to keep himself warm,
Will hide his head under his wing.
Poor thing!

Magpies

One for sorrow, two for joy,
Three for a girl, four for a boy,
Five for silver, six for gold,
Seven for a secret never to be told.

The Camel's Complaint

Canary-birds feed on sugar and seed,
Parrots have crackers to crunch;
And, as for the poodles, they tell me the noodles
Have chickens and cream for their lunch.
But there's never a question
About *my* digestion –
Anything does for me!

Cats, you're aware, can repose in a chair,
Chickens can roost upon rails;
Puppies are able to sleep in a stable,
And oysters can slumber in pails.
But no one supposes a poor camel dozes –
Any place does for me!

Lambs are enclosed where it's never exposed,
Coops are constructed for hens;
Kittens are treated to houses well-heated,
And pigs are protected by pens.
But a camel comes handy
Wherever it's sandy –
Anywhere does for me!

People would laugh if you rode a giraffe,
Or mounted the back of an ox;
It's nobody's habit to ride on a rabbit,
Or try to bestraddle a fox.
But as for a camel, he's ridden by families –
Any load does for me!

A snake is as round as a hole in the ground,
And weasels are wavy and sleek;
And no alligator could ever be straighter
Than lizards that live in a creek.
But a camel's all lumpy
And bumpy and humpy –
Any shape does for me!

It's Raining, It's Pouring

It's raining, it's pouring,
The old man is snoring;
He went to bed and bumped his head
And couldn't get up in the morning.

Blow, Wind, Blow

Blow, wind, blow! And go, mill, go!
That the miller may grind his corn;
That the baker may take it,
And into rolls make it,
And send us some hot in the morn.

Rain, Rain, Go Away

Rain, rain,
Go away,
Come again
Another day.

Sneeze on Monday

Sneeze on Monday, sneeze for danger;
Sneeze on Tuesday, kiss a stranger;
Sneeze on Wednesday, get a letter;
Sneeze on Thursday, something better;
Sneeze on Friday, sneeze for sorrow;
Sneeze on Saturday, see your sweetheart tomorrow.

Jackanory

I'll tell you a story
Of Jackanory,
And now my story's begun;
I'll tell you another
Of Jack his brother,
And now my story's done.

Little Wind

Little wind, blow on the hill-top;
Little wind, blow down the plain;
Little wind, blow up the sunshine;
Little wind, blow off the rain.

Little Bunny

Come, little bunny,
Say, "Good night".
There's lots to do
Before you turn out the light.

Collect all your toys
And put them away.
Kiss them good night –
It's the end of the day.

Hop in the bath
For a rinse and a scrub.
Play with the bubbles –
Rub-a-dub-dub!

Finish your story
And turn out the light.
Time to tuck you in warmly
And kiss you good night.

Mr Moon

Look through the window
At the moon shining bright.
Who can you see
In the twinkling starlight?

Up in the trees,
The grey doves coo.
Calling a friendly
"Good night" to you.

Good night, little squirrel.
Good night, little mouse.
Hurrying, scurrying to bed
In the house.

Listen to Owl calling,
"Who-whoo-whooo!"
While old Mr Moon
Watches over you.

Row, Row, Row Your Boat

Row, row, row your boat,
Gently down the stream,
Merrily, merrily, merrily, merrily,
Life is but a dream.

Jay-bird

Jay-bird, jay-bird, sittin' on a rail,
Pickin' his teeth with the end of his tail;
Mulberry leaves and calico sleeves —
All school teachers are hard to please.

Spin, Dame

Spin, dame, spin,
Your bread you must win;
Twist the thread and break it not,
Spin, dame, spin.

The Robin and the Wren

The robin and the wren,
They fought upon the porridge pan;
But before the robin got a spoon,
The wren had eaten the porridge down.

The Mouse's Lullaby

Oh, rock-a-bye, baby mouse, rock-a-bye, so!
When baby's asleep to the baker's I'll go,
And while he's not looking I'll pop from a hole,
And bring to my baby a fresh penny roll.

Bow-wow

Bow-wow, says the dog,
Mew, mew, says the cat,
Grunt, grunt, goes the hog,
And squeak goes the rat.
Tu-whu, says the owl,
Caw, caw, says the crow,
Quack, quack, says the duck,
And what cuckoos say you know.

Short Shooter

Miss Travers clapped her hands. "We have two new students today," she said. "Daniel? Sophie? Come up here, please."

Daniel and his sister walked under the basketball hoop and across the wooden floor. They stood beside Miss Travers and looked at their new classmates. The class stared back.

"This is Daniel and Sophie Lutz," Miss Travers said. "They're twins."

Miss Travers turned to Sophie. "We have a few sports teams at Park Street Primary School, Sophie. What's your favourite sport?" she asked.

"Football," Sophie said straight away.

A couple of girls in the front row smiled and gave her a 'thumbs up' sign.

"And how about you, Daniel?" Miss Travers asked.

Daniel held his breath. He looked at the hoop above his head. He'd give anything to play on the school team.

"I like basketball," he mumbled.

Miss Travers nodded, but quiet laughter and whispers came from some

of the class.

"You're too short for basketball!" a boy called.

Daniel's face felt hot.

"He's not!" Sophie said, defending her brother. "He practises with our big brother Mark all the time!"

Miss Travers turned to the boy who'd called out. "Get the ball bag please, Jason," she said. "We're playing basketball today."

The familiar sound of bouncing balls made Daniel feel calm. He stood in line with the others, shooting at the basket when it was his turn. Balls escaped into every corner of the room, but Daniel never missed a shot.

Miss Travers blew a whistle. "Jason and Daniel, come here please."

The two boys stood beside each other in front of the coach. Daniel was a head shorter than Jason.

"I've been watching you, Daniel," Miss Travers said. "I need another player for the basketball team." She bounced the ball to him. "If you can get a basket past Jason, you're on the team."

Jason laughed. "Ready, shorty?" he said. He spread his arms.

The class was silent as Daniel stood on his toes to peer over the taller boy's shoulder. The basket looked far away. He took

Mythical Monster

The monster lay in the mud at the bottom of the lake. She was sad. Everything had changed. Once, she'd been the most famous monster in the world. But now only a few people bothered to stand around waiting for a glimpse of her.

The monster knew what had gone wrong: she'd been too mean with her appearances. Once every twenty years just wasn't enough. People had got bored waiting.

She knew what to do. She had to make a splash! She swam across the lake, her spotted back breaking the surface. But when she lifted her neck, she saw that the shore was empty. In the distance there was a campsite, but the people there weren't looking towards the lake. They were outside their tents, reading newspapers and cooking supper. No one was interested in her.

She'd have to show herself properly, she decided. She swam to the shore and lumbered into the middle of the campsite.

A woman walked out of a tent. "Hey kids, that's a great costume," she cried, when she saw the monster. "Wherever did you get it? Now have a wash. Supper'll be ready soon."

As the monster was walking sadly back to the lake, a boy

76

came along. He screamed. "It's the monster!" he shouted.

"I wouldn't bother yourself with all that," said the monster to the astonished boy. "No one believes in me any more."

"That's terrible," said the boy. "We'll have to think of something that will get people's attention. I know – why don't I row out onto the lake and then pretend to be in trouble. Then you can rescue me."

The boy rowed himself out onto the lake, then deliberately pushed the oars away. "Help! I'm going to drown!" he cried.

The campers came running to the shore. Right on cue, the monster reared up out of the water. A great wave engulfed the boat, tossing the boy into the water.

"The monster's attacking my son!" cried a woman.

"That isn't what I had in mind," thought the monster. She plucked the boy from the water with her huge jaws.

"It's eating my son!" cried the woman.

Holding the boy in her mouth, the monster swam to the shore and put him down in front of his mother.

"The monster's saved my son!" cried the woman. "It's a hero!"

Cameras were flashing everywhere. "That's enough for me," the monster thought. She dived to the bottom of the lake. "I'll lay low for a while," she said to herself. "Just for another twenty years or so. A monster can only take so much attention, after all."

Smoky Smells Success

Smoky was a spook who haunted an ancient castle. And, being a ghost, Smoky could change shape at will.

"What shall I be next?" the spook wondered. "Headless the Horrible or Sir Percy, the Chain-Dragging Prisoner?" Smoky just loved inventing new spooky disguises. He only wished he had more visitors to try them out on.

One morning, Smoky heard a car pull up. A man and woman climbed out. They walked slowly around the castle walls, making notes, and looking very serious indeed.

"It's no use," said the man. "The castle's crumbling. We'll have to forget opening it to the public."

"If only we could raise enough money to repair it," replied the woman. Smoky froze. If his castle was pulled down, what would happen to him? Something had to be done!

As the visitors were returning to their car, they suddenly stopped and sniffed the air. There was a wonderful smell coming from the castle. The man pointed to what looked like a thin trail of steam floating by the entrance. It was Smoky, who had conjured up a delicious smell to tempt the visitors in.

Smoky led the man and the woman through the castle,

disguised as the thin trail of smoke. A secret door mysteriously swung open, and a narrow, cobweb-filled passage led the visitors to a hidden chamber and... a treasure chest!

"Unbelievable! There's more than enough money here to rebuild the castle ten times," cried the man.

Then the visitors shivered and glanced uneasily around.

"What about the ghosts people say live here?" said the man.

"Maybe they're friendly ghosts," said the woman. "But let's not stick around to find out!"

Soon after, workmen arrived to restore the castle. At first, they were nervous – but Smoky stayed out of sight.

The day before the castle was finally opened, the mayor came to look round. "It's such a pity the castle doesn't seem to be haunted after all," he said. "That would really put it on the map."

You can guess who was listening! Smoky chuckled with glee. He was more than happy to oblige! Quick as a flash he appeared as a court jester, then disappeared through the wall. The mayor almost jumped out of his skin!

After that Smoky had a wonderful time, trying out all his disguises on visitors who trembled with excitement as they searched the castle for ghosts. After all, everyone likes being a little bit scared now and then – don't you?

The Planet Where Time Goes Backwards

Far beyond our solar system,
In the outer reaches of space,
There's a planet where time goes backwards,
And it's the most peculiar place.

Cooks wash the dishes before the meal starts,
And unpeel potatoes, I'm told.
Your dinner goes into the oven
And comes out nice and cold.

Petrol pumps take the fuel out of cars,
And football's not much of a laugh:
The game ends with both teams at zero,
And they start by taking a bath.

You know something bad's going to happen,
When somebody starts to cry.
But the people get younger each day,
And they greet you by saying "Goodbye!"

A Whale of a Time

Did you hear the story of Wendy Bligh?
The remarkable whale who loved to fly?
It happened like this: she was sleeping one day,
When a hot-air balloonist flew her way.
He looked down below and spotted her hump,
"I'll land on that rock," said he, with a thump.
He tied up his balloon with a beautiful bow,
While Wendy slept on – she just didn't know.
Then a big tornado whirled over the sea,
It blew Wendy upwards as high as could be.
"What a wonderful feeling!" the whale cried in glee.
"I am floating above the sparkling blue sea!"
The hot-air balloonist took her for a spin;
She chatted to birds and waved her huge fin.
He dropped her back home at the end of the day.
"Oh thank you!" she smiled, and then swam away.

Would they be able to do it?

Amelia kicked the ball and Julia raced after it. She was fast, but not fast enough! A forward from Oakfield stole the ball and dribbled down the pitch.

Sophie sprinted after the forward. Her feet pounded into the grass. The forward's ponytail swished just out of reach. Sophie pushed her legs harder. She edged past and touched the ball with her toe. It spun to the side where Julia was ready.

Julia dribbled the ball back towards the Oakfield goal. Sophie raced down the pitch after her.

"Sophie!" Julia passed the ball to Sophie. Sophie dribbled it for a few steps but wasn't close enough to make a shot. She looked for a team mate who was clear.

"It's yours, Amelia!" Sophie kicked the ball towards the team captain and Amelia flicked it into the goal.

"Goal!" Miss Travers shouted. "Park Street wins!"

Sophie ran to help the team lift Amelia onto their shoulders. But then she stopped. The rest of the team were now running towards her!

"What are you doing?" Sophie asked, as the girls crowded round her, smiling.

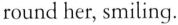

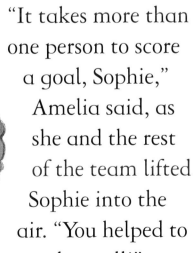

"It takes more than one person to score a goal, Sophie," Amelia said, as she and the rest of the team lifted Sophie into the air. "You helped to score them all!"

Brother and Sister

"*Sister*, sister, go to bed!
Go and rest your weary head."
Thus the prudent brother said.

"Do you want a battered hide,
Or scratches to your face applied?"
Thus his sister calm replied.

"Sister, do not raise my wrath.
I'd make you into mutton broth
As easily as kill a moth!"

The sister raised her beaming eye
And looked on him indignantly
And sternly answered, "Only try!"

Off to the cook he quickly ran.
"Dear Cook, please lend a frying-pan
To me as quickly as you can."

"And wherefore should I lend it you?"
"The reason, Cook, is plain to view.
I wish to make an Irish stew."

"What meat is in that stew to go?"
"My sister'll be the contents!" "Oh!"
"You'll lend the pan to me, Cook?" "No!"

Moral: Never stew your sister.

A Rat

There was a rat,
For want of stairs,
Went down a rope
To say his prayers.

Diddlety, Diddlety

Diddlety, diddlety, dumpty,
The cat ran up the plum tree;
Half a crown to fetch her down,
Diddlety, diddlety, dumpty.

Milking

Let down thy milk, old brown cow,
Let down thy milk and I'll give you a bow;
A bow, a coin and a golden key,
If thou wilt make sweet white milk for me.

Little Jack Jingle

Little Jack Jingle,
He used to live single:
But when he got tired of this kind of life,
He left off being single, and lived with his wife.

Way Down Yonder in the Maple Swamp

Way down yonder in the maple swamp
The wild geese gather and the ganders honk;
The mares kick up and the ponies prance;
The old sow whistles and the little pigs dance.

Follow My Bangalorey Man

Follow my Bangalorey Man,
Follow my Bangalorey Man;
I'll do all that ever I can
To follow my Bangalorey Man.
We'll borrow a horse, and steal a gig,
And round the world we'll do a jig,
And I'll do all that ever I can
To follow my Bangalorey Man!

Jack and the Beanstalk

Once upon a time there was a boy called Jack. He lived with his mother in a cottage. They were very poor.

One day, Jack's mother said, "We have no food left to eat and no money to buy it with. Take the cow to market and sell her."

So Jack took the cow to market. On the way, Jack met a very old man walking along the road.

"Where are you going?" asked the old man.

"I am going to market to sell the cow," said Jack.

The old man offered Jack five magic beans for the cow. Jack agreed and sold the cow, then took the beans home.

"I sold the cow for five magic beans," he told his mother.

"Five beans!" she said. She was cross! She threw the magic beans out of the window.

Then she sent Jack to bed without any supper.

In the morning, Jack woke up. He looked out of the window. There was a giant beanstalk. It went up, up into the sky.

Jack climbed up the beanstalk.

At the top, there was a giant castle. Jack knocked on the door. The door opened.

Jack went in. Everything in the castle was enormous. That was because a giant and his wife lived in the castle.

"Fee, fi, fo, fum!" said the giant. "I want my breakfast." Jack was afraid.

"You must hide," said the giant's wife, "or my husband will eat you."

Jack hid from the giant.

The giant sat down at the table. Then he put a hen on the table.

"Hen, lay an egg!" said the giant. The hen laid a golden egg.

"Here is your breakfast," said the giant's wife.

His wife gave him a very big breakfast.

The giant ate his breakfast. Then he felt very sleepy. "Time for my nap," he said.

Soon he was fast asleep.

"A golden egg!" said Jack. "I will take the hen. She will lay golden eggs and make us rich."

"Cluck!" said the hen. The giant woke up! Jack ran to the beanstalk. The giant ran after him.

But Jack got his axe and chopped down the beanstalk.

When the beanstalk fell to the ground, the giant came crashing down with it. That was the end of him!

Then the hen laid a golden egg.

And soon Jack and his mother weren't poor any more!

Helpful Little Digger

Little Yellow Digger was very excited.
It was his first day on the building site.
Chug! Chug! Chug!
Bulldozer was hard at work,
pushing piles of earth.

"Please may I help you?"
asked Little Yellow Digger.

"I don't need any help, thanks,"
replied Bulldozer. "Now watch out,
or you'll get knocked over!"

Dump Truck was working nearby.
"I don't need any help either, Little Yellow
Digger," he called.

Beep! Beep! Beep! Dump Truck's back lifted up.

"I'd better get out of the way quickly, before I'm buried in
sand," thought Little Yellow Digger. He felt very unhappy.
"Nobody wants my help on this site," he sighed.

Then Bulldozer and Dump Truck went *splutter* and *cough*.
"We've been working too hard!" they gasped. "We're running
out of fuel!"

"I'll help," cried Little Yellow Digger, and he sped towards
a pile of fuel drums. Little Yellow Digger took drums of fuel to
his two friends. Soon they were working again.

"You were good at helping after all," they cheered. "Hurrah
for Little Yellow Digger!"

The Incredible Centipede

I'm not just an ordinary centipede,
I live in a circus van.
I know all the top performers,
And I have a wonderful plan…

We'll reach a town, and as the sun goes down,
The folks will crowd the tent;
With music to thrill, they'll look at the line-up
And read with astonishment:

'Star of the show in the ring tonight,
And we hope he does succeed,
Is the enterprising, most surprising,
Incredible Centipede!'

The curtains will part and out I'll dart
And shake a leg or six,
Then in spangled tights I'll scale the heights
To perform my amazing tricks.

It will be so grand, in every land,
Royalty will want to be seen
Meeting the Incredible Centipede –
And I'll meet lots of kings and queens.

Chicken Licken

One day, Chicken Licken was scratching for food in the woods when, *Boink!* an acorn fell onto her head.

"Ruffle my feathers!" said Chicken Licken. "The sky is falling down. I must tell the King at once." And off she ran as fast she could.

On her way, Chicken Licken met Cocky Locky.

"I'm off to tell the King that the sky's falling down!" Chicken Licken said.

"Goodness!" clucked Cocky Locky. "I'd better come with you." And off they hurried.

On their way to see the King, Chicken Licken and Cocky Locky met Ducky Lucky.

"We're off to tell the King that the sky's falling down!" Chicken Licken said.

"Babbling brooks!" quacked Ducky Lucky. "Let's go. There's no time to lose."

They had just set off again, when they saw Goosey Loosey.

"We're off to tell the King the sky is falling down!" Chicken Licken said.

Goosey Loosey was very worried. "I'd better come too," she honked. So the four birds went along, until they met Foxy Loxy.

"Good day to you all!" said the crafty fox. "Where are you

going this fine day?"

Chicken Licken puffed up her chest importantly. "We're off to see the King," she announced. "The sky fell on my head in the woods. We must tell him at once."

Foxy Loxy grinned slyly. "Let me show you the quickest way there," he said, leading the way.

So Chicken Licken, Cocky Locky, Ducky Lucky and Goosey Loosey all followed Foxy Loxy until they came to a narrow, dark hole in the hillside.

"Follow me!" said sly Foxy Loxy. With that, he led Goosey Loosey, Ducky Lucky and Cocky Locky into his den. Chicken Licken was about to follow when all of a sudden there was a terrible honking and quacking and crowing from the hole!

"Oh no!" cried Chicken Licken. "Foxy Loxy has eaten Goosey Loosey, Ducky Lucky and Cocky Locky!"

She ran as fast as she could away from Foxy Loxy's den.

And Chicken Licken never did get to tell the King that the sky was falling down.

Zack's Birthday

Zack woke up early. He had been waiting for this day for weeks, and now it was here at last. It was his birthday!

Zack couldn't wait to open all his presents. He hoped one of them was the latest album by Alan and the Aliens, his favourite band.

He jumped out of bed and ran downstairs. Mum was in the kitchen oiling Tina the House Robot.

"Hello, Zack," said Mum. "Could you lay the breakfast table, please? Tina's not working this morning."

Zack couldn't believe his ears. No 'Happy Birthday'? "Where's Dad?" he asked.

"He's gone to work," said Mum. "He had to leave early because he's got a busy day."

Zelda ran into the kitchen. "I've got a school trip today!" she said. "My teacher told us to get to school early, because the space bus leaves at eight o'clock."

"We'd better rush!" said Mum. She handed Zack a carton of milk. "Get your own breakfast, Zack," she said. "I've got to take Zelda to school."

They had all forgotten his birthday!

Things didn't get better at Space School. Zack had all his worst lessons.

At home time, Zack's best friend Spud tried to cheer him up. "I'll race you!" he said. They bounced home on their space hoppers.

When Zack got home, Dad opened the front door.

"*Surprise!*" he said. All Zack's family were there, waiting to see him. There were balloons everywhere, and there was a huge pile of presents.

"We didn't really forget," said Mum, giving Zack a kiss. "Go on, birthday boy, open your presents!"

Zack ripped open an envelope. He thought it might be a birthday card from Aunt Alice, who lived on Mars.

"It's tickets to see Alan and the Aliens at the Moondust Superdrome tonight!" he cried.

"We're all going – Spud too," said Dad.

Zack grinned. It looked like this was going to be a fantastic birthday after all!

The Nasty Nice Spell

Of all the goblins that have ever played tricks upon the human world, Gordon Grizzle was surely the most cunning, mean and spiteful of them all. Every day, he crept around watching and waiting until he got the chance to spoil a person's happiness.

"That Gordon Grizzle will go too far one day!" warned Marcus Mildew, who was a very wise old goblin. The other goblins nodded and scratched their scruffy beards thoughtfully.

"But what can we do?" Marcus continued. "Aha! I think I might have an idea," he said, mysteriously.

The next day, when Gordon was snooping around looking for something really nasty to do, he overheard a conversation between two women.

"Young Annie's marrying Fred today," one of them was saying. "She's made a beautiful wedding gown. Of course, she had to make it from scraps of fabric, being so poor."

Gordon didn't hear the other woman's reply, because he was already scheming. He knew perfectly well why Annie was so poor. Why, wasn't it he himself who had turned her father's lottery winnings into autumn leaves and floated them down the river? Gordon grinned to himself. "Here's a chance to have some fun," he thought.

He could hear the wedding bells ringing and scampered off to the church, just in time to see Annie arrive. Gordon had to admit that she did look lovely in her pretty white dress. "Not for long!" he thought spitefully, as he cast his spell:

"Eye of bat and tooth of hag,
Make Annie's gown a tattered rag!"

Bam! The deed was done. Gordon giggled to himself. He heard the wedding guests gasp as they looked at Annie. "I bet she looks truly awful," he giggled. But then he peeped out from behind a pew, and to his utter astonishment, there was Annie wearing the most gorgeous silver gown he'd ever seen.

"That'll teach you!" said a familiar voice from behind him. It was Marcus Mildew. "I've been watching you, Gordon," he said. "I've seen your spiteful ways, spoiling everyone's fun. So I decided to spoil your fun, too! From now on, every time you cast a spell you'll find the opposite happens!"

Three Young Rats

Three young rats with black felt hats,
Three young ducks with white straw flats,
Three young dogs with curling tails,
Three young cats with demi-veils,
Went out to walk with two young pigs
In satin vests and sorrel wigs;
But suddenly it chanced to rain,
And so they all went home again.

Humpty Dumpty

Humpty Dumpty sat on a wall,
Humpty Dumpty had a great fall;
All the king's horses and all the king's men
Couldn't put Humpty together again.

We're All in the Dumps

We're all in the dumps,
For diamonds and trumps,
The kittens are gone to St Paul's,
The babies are bit,
The moon's in a fit,
And the houses are built without walls.

Tweedle-dum and Tweedle-dee

Tweedle-dum and Tweedle-dee
Agreed to have a battle,
For Tweedle-dum said Tweedle-dee
Had spoiled his nice new rattle.
Just then flew down a monstrous crow,
As big as a tar-barrel,
Which frightened both the heroes so,
They quite forgot their quarrel.

Daffy-Down-Dilly

Daffy-Down-Dilly
Has come up to town
In a yellow petticoat
And a green gown.

Little Tommy Tittlemouse

Little Tommy Tittlemouse
Lived in a little house;
He caught fishes
In other men's ditches.

Fiddlefingers

Captain Brassbuttons hummed happily and tapped his feet to a lively tune on board his pirate ship, *The Jolly Jig*.

The crew of *The Jolly Jig* preferred making music and having a merry time to pirating. After all, raiding ships was hard and dangerous work.

"'Tis a pity we don't have a fiddle player among us, cap'n," said Jake one day.

As he said this, a strong current suddenly picked the pirate ship up and whirled it away. When the ship finally came to rest, a wreck was drifting alongside the pirates.

"Stand by to board!" Brassbuttons cried to his men.

As Brassbuttons and his crew entered the crew's quarters of the wreck, he heard a terrible noise coming from a dark corner.

"Who goes there?" he called. Then, to his surprise, he saw a sailor lying in a hammock, snoring. There was a fiddle resting on the sailor's chest.

Brassbuttons poked the sailor with his cutlass and he woke with a start. "Who are you?" he gasped.

"We might ask the same of you," replied Brassbuttons.

"The crew called me Fiddlefingers, seeing as I was always playing this fiddle," said the sailor. "I've been stuck here, all alone, for more years than I can remember."

"A fiddle-player, you say? Then 'tis good fortune we found you!" boomed Brassbuttons.

No sooner had they welcomed Fiddlefingers aboard *The Jolly Jig* than he began to play. But what a shock! Instead of the tuneful harmony they had so been looking forward to hearing, he made a fearful, scratching screech.

And as he played, something strange started to happen. Around them, *The Jolly Jig* began to change in a fearful way. Huge, ragged holes appeared in the sails. Timbers began to creak eerily.

"Me fingers is going transparent!" cried Jake. The ship and its pirates were turning into a *ghost* ship! Yet, strangely, Fiddlefingers didn't seem to notice.

So that gloomy day spelled doom for *The Jolly Jig*. All that could be heard as the ghost ship drifted over the seas were the woeful wails of her poor suffering crew, as they tried to drown out the sound of the awful fiddling.

As for Fiddlefingers, he just smiled happily and played on, and on, and on...

The Fairy Ball

Late at night when the moon is bright,
And the air is soft and still,
Pixies peep and fairies creep,
And goblins roam at will.

Elves sneak out, and slink about,
Leprechauns come leaping.
Little sprites wave magic lights,
While the world is sleeping.

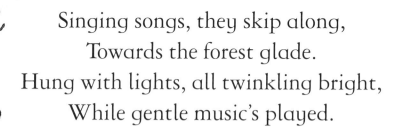

Singing songs, they skip along,
Towards the forest glade.
Hung with lights, all twinkling bright,
While gentle music's played.

They appear, from far and near,
A host of fairy folk.
This happy band dance hand in hand,
Beneath the magic oak.

Where Lies the Land?

Where lies the land to which the ship would go?
Far, far ahead, is all her seamen know.
And where the land she travels from? Away,
Far, far behind, is all that they can say.
On sunny noons upon the deck's smooth face,
Linked arm in arm, how pleasant here to pace;
Or, o'er the stern reclining, watch below
The foaming wake far widening as we go.

On stormy nights when wild north-westers rave,
How proud a thing to fight with wind and wave!
The dripping sailor on the reeling mast
Exults to bear, and scorns to wish it past.
Where lies the land to which the ship would go?
Far, far ahead, is all her seamen know.
And where the land she travels from? Away,
Far, far behind, is all that they can say.

Ice Cool Duel

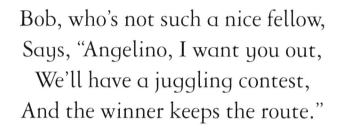

Angelino's Famous Ice Cream
Has a rival in town,
A juggling ice cream man called Bob,
Who'll bring his business down.

Bob, who's not such a nice fellow,
Says, "Angelino, I want you out,
We'll have a juggling contest,
And the winner keeps the route."

Angelino keeps his cool, though,
Knows that he will be just fine.
What goes up a plain old cone,
Comes down a lemon and lime.

Bob hates the thought of losing,
Reaches down towards his knees,
Juggles sixteen triple-dippers,
Tells Angelino, "Time to freeze!"

But Angelino's wise to Bob,
So he plays his final trick,
Bob falls, knocked out cold,
By a large vanilla brick!

Dino's

There's a prehistoric venue
That's open day and night.
With a megasaurus menu
For the larger appetite.

Try their Stegosaurus Steak
Or Brontosaurus Brunch,
A massive Mammoth Milkshake
Or the three-course Caveman's Lunch.

Triceratops call in to try
The Diplodocus Dips.
Pterodactyls leave the sky
For Dino's famous chips.

For the best in haute cuisine,
Nowhere could be finer.
It's the place you should be seen,
It's Dino's Downtown Diner.

So grant the dinosaur his wish
And come and join the queue.
You're sure to like his 'special' dish,
Why? Because it's *you*!

The Greedy Crows

It was milking time on Bluebell Farm and Farmer Jones was on his way to the cowshed. Mrs Jones, Farmer Jones's wife, came out of the farmhouse. She was wearing her smart clothes.

"I'm off to Sunnybridge market to do some shopping, Farmer Jones," she called to him. "Is there anything you need?"

"No, thanks!" said Farmer Jones. "You look very smart!"

"Thank you," said Mrs Jones. "You look like a scarecrow!"

"But I always dress like this," said Farmer Jones, looking down at his patched dungarees.

"That must be why you always look like a scarecrow," laughed Mrs Jones.

Later, Farmer Jones was in the milking parlour singing along to the radio when Max the sheepdog rushed in, barking.

"What is it?" asked Farmer Jones. As he followed Max out of the barn he could hear loud squawks coming from the cornfield. Farmer Jones began to run.

"Not those greedy crows again!" he cried. And, sure enough, a flock of crows was pecking away at Farmer Jones's lovely corn.

Farmer Jones raced around the field flapping his arms. But the crows just flew out of the way for a moment, then went back to their corn feast. "Can't catch us!" they cawed.

"I've got an idea!" said Farmer Jones suddenly.

"I know just what will get rid of those greedy crows!" And he ran off across the field and disappeared into his workshop. Soon the air was filled with a sound of hammering and sawing.

"Uh-oh!" said Pansy the pig. "It sounds like Farmer Jones is making something. And that usually means trouble."

Hours later, the workshop door swung open and a strange-looking machine rattled into sight.

"Introducing the Thingymajig!" cried Farmer Jones from behind the steering wheel.

The animals ran for cover as the Thingymajig crashed, banged and walloped its way towards the cornfield.

"Look out, you greedy crows!" chuckled Farmer Jones. "Here I come!"

He pulled a heavy lever and turned a huge dial. Out shot two tennis balls.

"Woof!" warned Max, as one tennis ball bounced on Pansy's bottom and landed in the water barrel. The second ball nearly hit the crows... but they just ducked.

"This isn't going to work!" thought Max.

"Take that!" Farmer Jones cried, fumbling with the lever. The Thingymajig began to rumble and rock. A spring flew into the air, spun around and knocked Farmer Jones into the duck pond. Then the Thingymajig collapsed into a heap.

"Caw! Caw! Caw!" laughed the crows.

Farmer Jones was soaked from head to toe. "It looks like I'll never get rid of those greedy crows," he said.

Back at the farmhouse, he emptied out his wellington boots, then took off his hat and dungarees. He was just hanging them on an old rake handle to dry when Mrs Jones arrived home.

"Oh dear!" she said. "Whatever happened to you?"

"It's a long story," said Farmer Jones. "But the long and short of it is I fell into the duck pond."

"It's a good thing I bought you these, then," smiled Mrs Jones. And she gave Farmer Jones a bag. Inside were a new hat, shirt, dungarees and wellington boots.

Farmer Jones looked at his new clothes and looked at his old clothes. Then he remembered what Mrs Jones had said that morning. He grabbed both sets of clothes.

"I've got an idea!" he shouted.

Five minutes later, Farmer Jones came out of his workshop carrying a scarecrow wearing his old clothes.

Max and Farmer Jones carried the scarecrow down to the cornfield. The crows took one look at the scarecrow...

... and disappeared in fright!

Yankee Doodle

Yankee Doodle went to town,
Riding on a pony;
He stuck a feather in his hat,
And called it macaroni.
Yankee Doodle fa, so, la,
Yankee Doodle dandy,
Yankee Doodle fa, so, la,
Buttermilk and brandy.

Yankee Doodle went to town
To buy a pair of trousers,
He swore he could not see the town
For so many houses.
Yankee Doodle fa, so, la,
Yankee Doodle dandy,
Yankee Doodle fa, so, la,
Buttermilk and brandy.

Cat of Cats

I am the cat of cats. I am
The everlasting cat!
Cunning, and old, and sleek as jam,
The everlasting cat!
I hunt the vermin in the night –
The everlasting cat!
For I see best without the light –
The everlasting cat!

The Hare and the Tortoise

Once upon a time there was a hare who was always boasting about how fast he was.

One day, much to everyone's surprise, after Hare had been boasting even more than normal, Tortoise said, "Okay, Hare. I'll race you."

"Whaaaaat?" laughed Hare. "You've got to be joking." He laughed so much that he fell to his knees and thumped the floor with his fist.

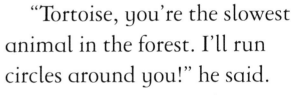

"Tortoise, you're the slowest animal in the forest. I'll run circles around you!" he said.

There was a buzz of excitement in the forest the next morning.

"On your marks, get set… go!" cried the starting fox.

And Hare flew off at high speed, leaving a cloud of smoke where he had just

stood. The tortoise trudged behind much, much, much more slowly.

Hare decided to take a quick look behind to see where the slow tortoise was. When he saw that Tortoise was far, far away, he decided to stop for breakfast. He feasted on some juicy carrots. Then he lay on his back, fiddled with his ears and yawned.

"This is just too easy," he said. "I think I'll have forty winks and catch up with him later." Soon he was fast asleep.

Tortoise plodded on and on. He got to where Hare was lying, fast asleep, and plodded past. He plodded on and on. Hare slept, on and on.

Suddenly Hare awoke with a jolt. He could just see Tortoise in the distance, plodding slowly and carefully towards the finish line.

"Noooooooo!" cried Hare. He leapt to his feet and charged towards the finish as fast as he could. But he was too late. Tortoise was over the line before him. Hare had been beaten.

After that, whenever anyone heard Hare boasting about his speed they reminded him about the day Tortoise beat him.

"Slow and steady won the race," they would say, laughing.

And all Hare could do was smile because, after all, they were quite right.

Seal Song

You mustn't swim till you're six weeks old,
Or your head will be sunk by your heels;
And summer gales and killer whales
Are bad for baby seals.
Are bad for baby seals, dear rat,
As bad as bad can be;
But splash and grow strong,
And you can't be wrong,
Child of the Open Sea!

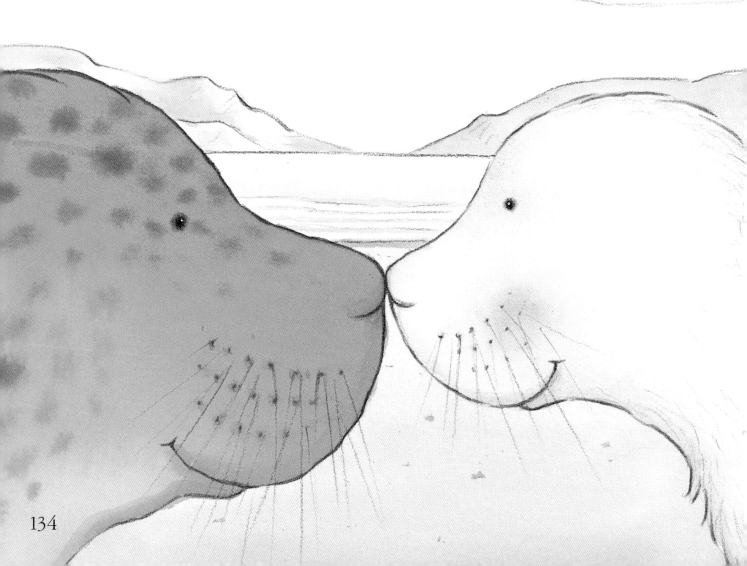

Pirate Song

Fifteen men on the dead man's chest –
Yo ho ho and a bottle of rum!
Drink and the devil had done for the rest –
Yo ho ho and a bottle of rum!

Mad Monsters

Squeak! Squeak!
Monster fun!
Orange tickles everyone!

Squeak! Squeak!
Clumsy Green
Has the biggest feet you've ever seen!

Squeak! Squeak!
Silly Red,
Hiding underneath the bed!

Squeak! Squeak!
Snoozy Yellow,
Fast asleep, the lazy fellow!

Squeak! Squeak!
What a noise!
Purple plays with all his toys.

Squeak! Squeak!
Pretty Pink!
She looks lovely, don't you think?

Mystery Monster

You wake with a start,
In the still of the night,
With your toes all exposed,
And your quilt pulled up tight.

You open your eyes,
You stare through the gloom,
Strange shadows loom large,
On the walls of your room.

You hear a loud creak,
As the monster draws near,
And the more that you listen,
The more that you hear.

Then you see its weird shape,
At the end of your bed,
With long skinny legs,
And a great lumpy head.

So you switch on the light,
And you whisper, "Who's there?"
But it's only your clothes,
Hanging over the chair!

Perfect Turns

"How's your swimming training going?"
Sophie asked her brother, as she scooped
up a spoonful of breakfast cereal.

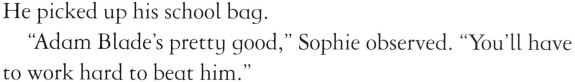

Daniel shrugged. "I'm not getting
any faster and the school swimming
gala is only three weeks away."
He picked up his school bag.

"Adam Blade's pretty good," Sophie observed. "You'll have
to work hard to beat him."

"I know," Daniel replied as he left for the pool. "He trains
every morning, like me."

Sophie carried on eating her
breakfast. Daniel had set his
heart on winning the 200-metre
freestyle race. He wanted the
prize: four free tickets to see the
new *Pirates* film. But so did
Adam Blade.

Daniel shivered as he stood with
his toes over the edge of the pool. Adam was already speeding
through the water.

Daniel took a deep breath and dived in. He swam slowly at
first. As his muscles grew warm he began to swim faster. He
passed Adam a few times, but, just as often, Adam passed him.

"Daniel!" a muffled voice shouted.

Daniel finished his lap and looked up. It was Sophie. "What are you doing here?" he asked.

Sophie dangled her feet in the water. "I decided to watch you training," she replied.

Daniel sighed. "I think I'm losing time in my turns," he said.

Sophie looked over at Adam. She watched as he came to the end of a lap, flipped over and pushed away from the wall. "Wow," she said. "Did you see that?"

Daniel watched Adam swim to the other side of the pool. "See what?" he asked.

"Adam's turns are perfect," Sophie told him. "He hardly slows down. Watch."

Adam performed another rapid turn and then headed towards them.

Daniel was quiet as he studied Adam's swimming stroke. "You know, if he kept his legs straighter and pointed his toes more, he would swim faster."

Sophie nodded. "And if you improved your turns, you'd make better time too."

Adam reached the end of the pool.

Daniel cupped his hands around his mouth.

Welcome to the Haunted House!

Step in through the rusty gates –
Be quiet as a mouse.
We're going to sneak, and take
A peek, inside the Haunted House!

Upstairs in the dusty bedrooms
Skeletons are getting dressed.
Vampires brush their hair and teeth.
All the spooks must look their best!

An empty suit of shiny armour
Is clanking loudly down the hall,
To a party in the ballroom –
It's the Spooks' Secret Ball!

So while the party's in full swing,
Be quiet as a mouse.
Tiptoe out while you still can –
Escape the Haunted House!

Five Little Monkeys

Five little monkeys walked along the shore;
One went a-sailing,
Then there were four.
Four little monkeys climbed up a tree;
One of them tumbled down,
Then there were three.
Three little monkeys found a pot of glue;
One got stuck in it,
Then there were two.
Two little monkeys found a currant bun;
One ran away with it,
Then there was one.
One little monkey cried all afternoon,
So they put him in an aeroplane
And sent him to the moon.

Howls and Owls

"*Owwww!*" A horrible howl rang out through the darkness. Beneath the moon, Hairy the Horrible Hound sat staring at his paws. He had been howling away all evening. He wanted someone to talk to, someone to play with. But because he was a ghost hound no one would come near.

The moon shone between the clouds and lit up the ruined manor house on top of the hill. The people who once lived there had fled years ago. Now it was just the haunt of Shiver, an old ghost.

Shiver was resting. At the first sound of Hairy's howls, he groaned. "Hairy's dreadful noise goes right through my skull!" he cried. "Something must be done!"

"Who's Hairy?" a voice above Shiver asked. An owl flitted through a hole in the roof.

"Hairy is the ghost hound who howls horribly outside in the lane," said Shiver. "I wish he would stop."

"He might, if you ask him nicely," blinked the owl.

"M-me? Face Hairy the Horrible Hound?" breathed Shiver.

"Well, someone should!" said the

owl. "I only flew in yesterday and I must say, I'm tired of that howling already! I suppose I'll have to do it myself."

Soon the owl was back. But this time he wasn't alone! There was a padding of paws on the front steps, then the door swung open on its creaky hinges.

"Yikes! Time I disappeared!" trembled Shiver. But it was too late! In swept the owl, followed by the ghostly hound.

"Hairy told me he only howls because he's lonely," said the owl. "He chases anything that moves, too, in the hope of finding a friend! If you want my advice, you should let him come and live here. What better than a ghostly guard dog?"

"I promise I'd never howl again," pleaded Hairy, hopefully.

"You can lie beside my old bed, Hairy," smiled Shiver, who wasn't the least bit nervous now.

And so Hairy the Horrible Hound found a home at last.

But if Shiver had hoped for some peace and quiet, he was to be sadly disappointed. For if Hairy wasn't playfully pulling the sheets off Shiver, he was leaping onto his lap for company.

Slowly, though, Shiver grew to like things being more lively. Which was just as well, or Hairy might have had to start howling again!

Tumbling

In jumping and tumbling we spend the whole day,
Till night by arriving has finished our play.
What then? One and all, there's no more to be said,
As we tumbled all day, so we tumble to bed.

Lie a-Bed

Lie a-bed,
Sleepy head,
Shut up eyes, bo-peep;
Till day-break
Never wake:–
Baby, sleep.

There Was a Crooked Man

There was a crooked man, and he went a crooked mile,
He found a crooked sixpence against a crooked stile;
He bought a crooked cat, which caught a crooked mouse,
And they all lived together in a little crooked house.

Three Wise Men of Gotham

Three wise men of Gotham
Went to sea in a bowl:
And if the bowl had been stronger,
My song would have been longer.

I Hear Thunder

I hear thunder, I hear thunder,
Hark! don't you? Hark! don't you?
Pitter, patter raindrops, pitter, patter raindrops,
I'm wet through, I'm wet through.

Pop Goes the Weasel

Half a pound of tuppenny rice,
Half a pound of treacle.
That's the way the money goes,
Pop! goes the weasel.

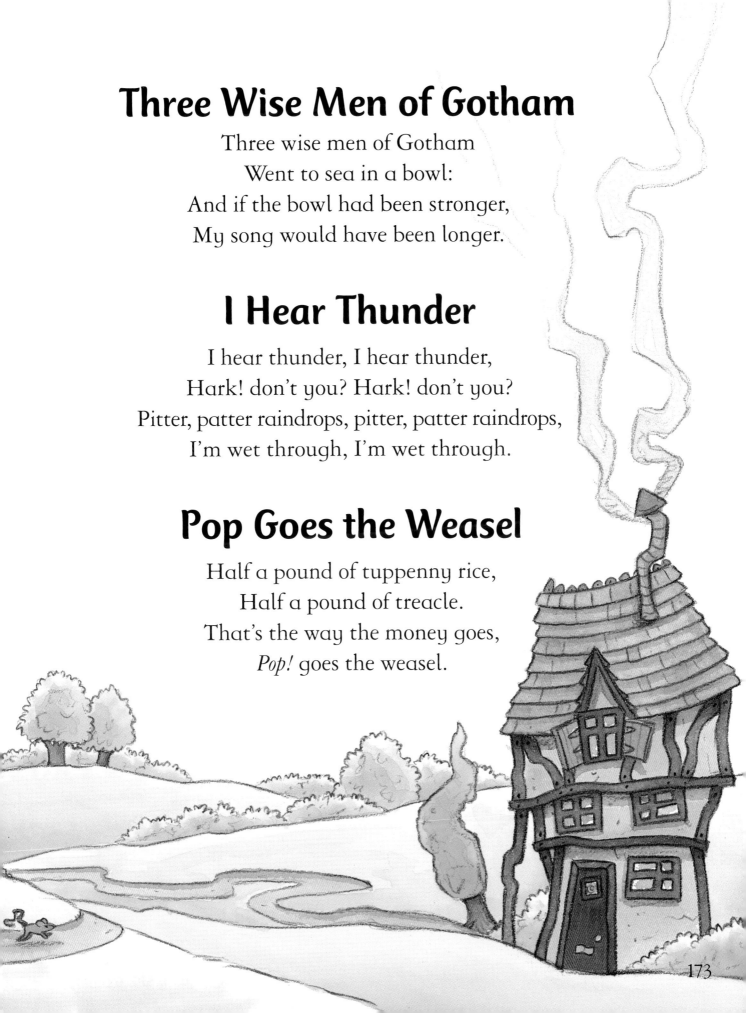

Storm Rescue

One windy day there was a big black cloud over the farm. There was a flash of lightning and a loud rumble of thunder.

"Come on, Patch," cried Farmer Fred. "We'll get the animals into the barn."

"Neigh!" said Harry Horse, trying to help. He plodded after Farmer Fred.

"Oh, dear," sighed Harry Horse. "I'm too slow for herding cows and sheep. Perhaps I can help the ducks and hens."

Harry Horse stamped his hoof to nudge the hens towards the barn. But his stamping hooves frightened the hens.

"I'm too big," sighed Harry. "I'm just a useless old horse."

Soon, the animals were safe in the barn. Harry Horse noticed that Polly Pig and her piglets were missing. He neighed and stamped his hoof.

Farmer Fred looked around. "Whizzing hurricanes!" he cried. "Polly and her piglets are missing."

Farmer Fred and the animals raced to Hog Hollow. The storm had blown a tree across the entrance of Polly Pig's sty.

"Polly and her piglets are trapped!" said Farmer Fred. "We'll have to pull that tree out of the way. The tractor won't fit through the gate. But never fear, I've an idea!"

Farmer Fred disappeared into his workshop.

Later, he appeared, grinning. "This," he said, "is the new Mobile Hand-saw. It will cut through the tree in no time!"

Farmer Fred wheeled the Mobile Hand-saw to the pig sty. He flipped a switch and it roared into life. It began to rattle and shake. Then, with a loud *ping* the elastic broke.

"Let's try to lift the tree out of the way," said Farmer Fred.

Farmer Fred and the animals pushed and pulled. But it was no good – the tree wouldn't budge.

"Woof! Woof!" barked Patch, pulling at Harry's old harness.

"Hold on, I've had an idea!" cried Fred. "I know who can help me drag that tree out of the way."

Farmer Fred quickly harnessed Harry Horse. He attached some rope to the harness, and tied the rope around the tree.

"Heave!" cried Farmer Fred. Harry dug in his hooves and heaved. The tree began to slide away from the sty.

At last, Polly and her piglets were free.

"What a useful horse!" cried all the animals.

Harry Horse neighed happily. He was a useful horse, after all!

Hark At the Robbers

Hark at the robbers going through,
Through, through, through; through, through, through;
Hark at the robbers going through, my fair lady.

What have the robbers done to you,
You, you, you; you, you, you?
What have the robbers done to you, my fair lady?

Stole my gold watch and chain,
Chain, chain, chain; chain, chain, chain;
Stole my gold watch and chain, my fair lady.

How many pounds will set us free,
Free, free, free; free, free, free?
How many pounds will set us free, my fair lady?

A hundred pounds will set you free,
Free, free, free; free, free, free;
A hundred pounds will set you free, my fair lady.

My Father He Died

My father he died, but I can't tell you how,
He left me six horses to drive in my plough:
  With my wing wang waddle oh,
    Jack sing saddle oh,
    Blowsey boys bubble oh,
      Under the broom.

I sold my six horses and I bought me a cow,
    I'd fain have made a fortune,
      But did not know how:
  With my wing wang waddle oh,
    Jack sing saddle oh,
    Blowsey boys bubble oh,
      Under the broom.

I sold my cow, and I bought me a calf;
    I'd fain have made a fortune,
      But lost the best half:
  With my wing wang waddle oh,
    Jack sing saddle oh,
    Blowsey boys bubble oh,
      Under the broom.

177

Surprise Sports Star

"Oh, no! We've got Jasmine," Jason whispered to Daniel and Sophie. "She's hopeless." The class was about to play basketball.

Sophie frowned. "Give Jasmine a chance," she said.

Staring at her shoes, Jasmine walked over to her team.

Miss Travers held up the basketball. "Ready?" she called. Then she blew her whistle.

During the game, Sophie saw Jasmine shy away whenever the ball came near.

But then, near the end of the game, Daniel yelled, "Jasmine! You're closest to the net!" He threw the ball towards her.

"Catch it!" yelled Jason.

Jasmine ran forward, holding out her arms.

Sophie held her breath.

The ball slipped through Jasmine's hands and bounced off the ground.

Sammy on the other team grabbed it and headed off to the other end of the court. He steered the ball up into the air and it dropped neatly into the net.

"Score!" his team shouted.

Miss Travers blew her

whistle. The game was over.

Sophie watched Jasmine trudge from the sports hall. She hurried to catch up with her. "Cheer up, Jasmine," she said. "It's supposed to be fun."

"I know," Jasmine replied quietly. "But I'm hopeless." She shrugged and walked away.

"Did you hear about the charity fun run?" Daniel asked Sophie as they walked home. "You collect sponsors and run laps around the school track."

Just then, Jasmine sprinted round the corner with her older brother. Both of them carried bags full of newspapers.

Sophie stopped, her eyes wide. "Look!" she said. "See how fast Jasmine's running!"

"Maybe she should enter the fun run," said Daniel.

Sophie nodded and began running after Jasmine. "Hey! Jasmine!" she called.

Jasmine stopped, allowing Sophie and Daniel to catch up.

"You're so fast!" Sophie panted.

Jasmine shrugged. "We run to get the paper round finished quickly," she said.

The Three Little Pigs

Once upon a time there were three little pigs. One day the three little pigs set off to find new homes.

Soon the three little pigs saw a pile of straw.

"I'll build my house of straw," said the first little pig.

The two little pigs walked on. They saw a big pile of sticks underneath an oak tree.

"I'll build my house of sticks," said the second pig.

The third little pig walked on. He saw a pile of bricks.

"I'll build a strong house of bricks," said the third little pig.

It took the third little pig a long time to build his house. His brothers laughed at him for working so hard. But the house of bricks was very strong.

The very next day, a big bad wolf called at the house of straw.

"Little pig, little pig, let me come in," said the wolf.

"Not by the hair of my chinny chin chin!" said the first little pig. So the wolf huffed and he puffed and he blew the house down.

The little pig ran away

and hid with his brother in the house of sticks.

The next day, the big bad wolf called at the house of sticks.

"Little pig, little pig, let me come in," he said.

"Not by the hair of my chinny chin chin!" said the second little pig. So the wolf huffed and he puffed and he blew the house down.

The two little pigs ran away and hid with their brother in the house of bricks.

The next day, the big bad wolf called at the house of bricks.

"Little pig, little pig, let me come in," said the wolf.

"Not by the hair of my chinny chin chin!" said the third little pig. So the wolf huffed and he puffed. But he couldn't blow the house down.

The big bad wolf was very cross. "I'm coming down the chimney to eat you!" he cried.

The third little pig made a fire under the chimney. Then he put a pot of water on the fire.

The big bad wolf climbed down the chimney and *Splash!* He fell into the pot of hot water.

"Help! Help!" cried the wolf. He jumped out of the pot and ran out of the house.

And he was never seen again.

Birthday Surprise

It was Patch the sheepdog's birthday on Bluebell Farm.

"Fred, it's your job to decorate the barn for the surprise birthday party," said Jenny. "I'm going to bake the cake."

"No problem!" said Farmer Fred.

Farmer Fred sent Patch up to the top field to count sheep, then he and the animals began to decorate the barn. They piled all the presents on a bale of hay and hung up a big banner. Then Farmer Fred started blowing up balloons. He puffed and puffed. It was taking *ages*!

"Never fear, I've an idea!" he cried, and disappeared into his workshop. Not long after the door swung open and out stepped Farmer Fred pushing a strange-looking machine.

"This," he said proudly, "is the Puffomatic Balloon-blower. All I need to do is flick this switch and we'll have those balloons blown up before you can say *Party Poppers*!"

Farmer Fred pulled some balloons over the neck of the machine and flicked a switch. Within seconds the balloons had reached their full size.

"There," said Farmer Fred.

But the Balloon-blower didn't stop. The balloons grew bigger and bigger until suddenly…

BANG! They burst. Bales of hay flew this way and that. All the animals ran out of the barn as fast as they could.

Patch raced down from the field. "Woof! Woof!" he barked. "What's going on?"

Patch couldn't see Farmer Fred anywhere. He went into the barn. There were bits of machine and bales of hay all over the place. But Farmer Fred was nowhere to be seen.

"Woof! Woof!" barked Patch, as he spotted Farmer Fred's hat sticking out from beneath a bale of hay. Patch pushed the bale of hay out of the way. And there was Farmer Fred.

"Woof! Woof!" barked Patch, licking Farmer Fred's face.

"Thanks," laughed Farmer Fred. "I think that perhaps the Puffomatic…err… thingy could do with a bit more work."

Just then, Jenny came into the barn with a bone-shaped cake.

"Ah, you're all here," she smiled, looking around. "And I can see that you've been busy decorating. Now we can start the surprise birthday party."

"Happy Birthday, Patch!" shouted everyone.

I Love Sixpence

I love sixpence, pretty little sixpence,
I love sixpence better than my life;
I spent a penny of it, I spent another,
And I took fourpence home to my wife.

Oh, my little fourpence, pretty little fourpence,
I love fourpence better than my life;
I spent a penny of it, I spent another,
And I took twopence home to my wife.

Oh, my little twopence, my pretty little twopence,
I love twopence better than my life;
I spent a penny of it, I spent another,
And I took nothing home to my wife.

Oh, my little nothing, my pretty little nothing,
What will nothing buy for my wife?
I have nothing, I spend nothing,
I love nothing better than my wife.

From a Railway Carriage

Faster than fairies, faster than witches,
Bridges and houses, hedges and ditches;
And charging along like troops in a battle,
All through the meadows the horses and cattle:
All of the sights of the hill and the plain
Fly as thick as driving rain;
And ever again, in the wink of an eye,
Painted stations whistle by.

Here is a child who clambers and scrambles,
All by himself and gathering brambles;
Here is a tramp who stands and gazes;
And there is the green for stringing the daisies!
Here is a cart run away in the road
Lumping along with man and load;
And here is a mill, and there is a river:
Each a glimpse and gone for ever!

The Science Project

Jed's mum was on the phone. Jed sat at the top of the stairs, listening carefully.

"Mission understood, sir," said Mum. "You can rely on me." She put down the phone and went into the kitchen to finish making dinner.

Jed crept into Mum's office. She had left her work on the computer screen. It told him all about her new mission. Jed smiled.

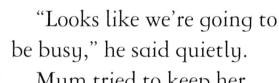

"Looks like we're going to be busy," he said quietly.

Mum tried to keep her job a secret from Jed, but he knew she was a special agent. A spy! She worked for Unit X, a top-secret organization used by the government to sort out its trickiest problems.

Jed had a secret of his own: he sometimes helped Mum on her missions. But he made sure she never found out.

Jed looked at the computer screen and read about the new mission. An important new invention had gone missing: a new energy-saving fuel. Mum had to find it and return it to the Winger Science Centre – as soon as possible!

"Dinner's ready, Jed!" Mum called.

Jed turned away from the computer and went downstairs.

"Your favourite!" said Mum, passing him a plateful of chicken curry. "Have you got any homework this weekend?" she asked.

Suddenly, Jed had an idea. "I have a science project on pollution," he replied. "My teacher said the Winger Science Centre has a good exhibition. Can we go there, please?" Jed held his breath. Would Mum take the bait?

Mum looked surprised. "What a coincidence!" she said. "I have to visit the Winger Science Centre tomorrow afternoon. You can come with me."

The next afternoon, Mum pulled into the Winger Science Centre car park. "I'll go and talk to the manager while you look at the exhibition," she said. "Meet you in an hour."

"OK," Jed replied. But as Mum walked away, Jed ran off around the side of the building.

Seeing an open window on the ground floor, Jed climbed through it. He found himself in a long corridor. Suddenly he heard a familiar voice. Mum!

Jed quickly hid behind a big pot plant as Mum turned the corner, talking to the research centre manager.

"Here's my office," said the manager, opening a door.

Jed breathed a sigh of relief as they disappeared inside.

Hot Cross Buns

Hot cross buns!
Hot cross buns!
One-a-penny, two-a-penny,
Hot cross buns!
If you have no daughters,
Give them to your sons,
One-a-penny, two-a-penny,
Hot cross buns!

Wash Hands

Wash, hands, wash,
Daddy's gone to plough;
If you want your hands wash'd,
Have them wash'd now.

Willie Wastle

I, Willie Wastle,
Stand on my castle,
An' a' the dogs o' your toon,
Will no' drive Willie Wastle down.

Richard Dick

Richard Dick upon a stick,
Sampson on a sow,
We'll ride away to Colley fair
To buy a horse to plough.

Parliament Soldiers

High diddle ding, did you hear the bells ring?
The parliament soldiers are gone to the king.
Some they did laugh, and some they did cry,
To see the parliament soldiers go by.

Oats and Beans

Oats and beans and barley grow,
Oats and beans and barley grow,
Do you or I or anyone know,
How oats and beans and barley grow?

First the farmer sows his seeds,
Then he stands and takes his ease,
Stamps his feet and claps his hands,
Turns around to view the land.

The Dog and the Ball

It was the summer holidays. Ross and Jane were camping with their families near the beach.

"Let's play ball on the beach today!" said Jane.

Ross got a ball from his tent and they went to play on the beach. The sun was shining brightly and the waves were crashing onto the sand.

Ross threw the ball to Jane. "Catch, Jane!" he called.

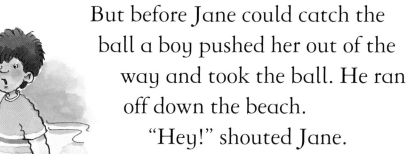

But before Jane could catch the ball a boy pushed her out of the way and took the ball. He ran off down the beach.

"Hey!" shouted Jane.

"Come back!" shouted Ross. "That's our ball!"

Ross and Jane ran after the boy, but they couldn't catch up with him. Soon he had disappeared behind the rocks at the end of the beach.

Then they heard a cry mixed up with some loud barking.
"Help me! Help me!"
"Woof! Woof! Woof!"
Ross and Jane peered over the rocks. It was the boy who had taken their ball. He was lying on the ground and on top of him was a big, shaggy, brown and white dog.

"Get him off me," cried the boy. "I'm scared!"

Jane looked at the dog. Its tail was wagging and its tongue was hanging out. It didn't look scary at all, she thought.

"The dog only wants to play with you, you know," said Jane.

"Get him off me!" wailed the boy.

"Okay, give me the ball," said Ross to the boy.

The boy gave Ross the ball. Ross leant back and then threw it far down the beach.

"Fetch!" he called to the dog.

"Woof!" barked the dog excitedly, racing off down the beach after the ball.

The boy jumped up and ran off towards the campsite. He didn't even say thank you.

"What a mean boy," said Jane.

The dog came racing back with the ball in his mouth. He put it at Ross's feet and waited for Ross to throw it again.

"Never mind," said Ross. "We have our ball."

"And we have a new friend," laughed Jane, patting the dog.

"Woof!" said the dog.

Hide-and-seek

It was playtime at school. The animals were playing hide-and-seek. Lucy Lion counted to ten. The animals ran to hide.

"Ninety-nine... One hundred! I'm coming!" called Lucy.

Lucy looked high and low. She couldn't find Helga Hippo.

Lucy looked high and low. She couldn't find Mikey Monkey.

Lucy looked high and low. She couldn't find Jed Giraffe.

"Where is everybody?" Lucy wondered. She kept looking. She looked and looked and looked until she started to get tired.

When the bell rang for the end of playtime the animals came out of their hiding places.

"Where's Lucy?" asked Mrs Beak, the teacher.

They looked high and low for Lucy. Helga Hippo couldn't find her. Mikey Monkey couldn't find her. Jed Giraffe couldn't find her.

Then Mrs Beak found her. Lucy had given up. She was fast asleep under a tree!

The Diplodocus couldn't hear him. Tony's shouts sounded like tiny, faraway squeaks. However, it had spotted the bright orange raft and made straight for it.

Tony fired a round of darts from his stun gun at the huge creature and waited for it to keel over.

The Diplodocus just shook itself lazily and looked a little bit annoyed. It studied the tiny red-faced man that was irritating it, then bent down and seized Tony in its mouth.

But the Diplodocus, being a plant-eater, didn't eat Tony. Instead, it tossed him away. Then it picked up the raft and hurled it after him.

Tony flew out of the valley and over the hills beyond.

Luckily for him, he landed safely, with an almighty splash, in a distant lagoon.

A few moments later, his raft hit the water right beside him. Tony paddled across that lagoon to the town on its banks as fast as he could go. Then he hailed a taxi to the airport, boarded a plane and never, ever went back to the valley.

Meeting the Diplodocus changed Tony forever. He shut down his circus and released all the animals safely back into the wild.

And the herd of Diplodocus lived happily ever after.

Lonely Whale

"I wish I had someone to play with," said Whale. He was splashing around by himself in the sea.

"Hello, Whale! Want to play?" asked Seahorse, jumping out from under the rocks. But Seahorse was so small, Whale didn't hear him.

Two dolphins began leaping to and fro across Whale's back. "Play with us, Whale!" they cried. But Whale was so big, he didn't notice them.

Then three fish floated by. "Play with us, Whale!" they said. But the fish were so far away, Whale didn't see them.

Whale found Eel wriggling around the rocks. "I'd like to wriggle like that," said Whale. "But I'm so big and clumsy, I can't do anything," said Whale, sadly.

"But you're the biggest animal in the sea. Everyone loves you," said Eel. "Have a look behind you!"

Whale turned around and saw all the fish in the sea!

"Please play, Whale," they cried.

"I'm the luckiest whale in the whole world!" said Whale, and he swam off to join his friends.

Sssssh!

It was the middle of the night. All of a sudden, Kitten's tummy began to rumble.

"I'm really hungry!" said Kitten. "I've just got to go to the kitchen and find something to eat."

Kitten tried to quietly jump to the floor, but he landed on Puppy's tail instead.

"*Ow!*" cried Puppy.

"*Sssssh!*" whispered Kitten. "You'll wake everyone up!"

Kitten tiptoed down the hall…

"*Boo!*" shouted Rabbit, hopping up.

"*Sssssh!*" whispered Kitten. "You'll wake everyone up!"

Kitten crept through the living room and was startled by a noise under the sofa.

"Who's there?" asked Kitten, nervously.

"*Squeak! Squeak!*" squeaked Hamster.

"*Sssshh!*" whispered Kitten. "You'll wake everyone up!"

"*Meeeow!*" howled Kitten when he reached the kitchen at last. There was a fat little mouse eating out of his bowl!

"*Crash!*" went the bowl, and the dishes, and the saucepans, as Kitten chased the mouse all over the kitchen.

And after all that loud noise, who do you think woke up? Everyone!

The Shopping Trip

"I wish I could buy a new bike," said Eddie, gazing into the bike shop window. "Mine's useless."

"Me too," said Josh. "But neither of us has any money."

They both sighed.

Eddie grabbed Josh's arm. "I know!" he said. "We could make our own money, running errands!"

"Try Mrs Cole next door," said Eddie's mum, when they told her their plan. "She might have a few jobs you could do."

Mrs Cole gave Eddie and Josh a huge shopping list. "Make sure you don't forget anything!" she snapped. Mrs Cole was always bad-tempered.

Eddie and Josh spent ages at the supermarket finding everything on the list. They paid at the checkout and stared at the pile of heavy bags.

"How are we going to carry all this?" Josh asked.

"Wait here!" Eddie told Josh. And he raced off.

Eddie returned with his baby sister's pram and Rusty, his dog.

"Put the shopping in the pram, Josh," he said, tying Rusty's lead to the pram. "Rusty can pull the shopping home for us."

But as Josh put the last bag in the pram, Rusty spotted a cat and darted after it.

"Quick!" yelled Eddie. "Follow that pram!"

As Rusty and the pram passed Mrs Cole's house, Rusty dodged a lamp post and *Crash!* The pram smashed right into it.

Five big shopping bags flew through the air and then landed with a terrible clatter.

Mrs Cole rushed out. "Tidy up this mess!" she shouted. "And then buy me some more shopping with your own money!" She marched back into her house and slammed the door.

Then a window opened. It was Mr Cole. "That chase was the funniest thing!" he said, laughing. "Come over here."

The boys went over to the window. "Don't tell Mrs Cole I paid you," he whispered, handing them the money. "And don't worry about the cost of the shopping, either. Seeing something so funny was worth it!"

He smiled. "But I think I'll go shopping myself – in the car!"

Poor Old Robinson Crusoe!

Poor old Robinson Crusoe!
Poor old Robinson Crusoe!
They made him a coat of an old nanny goat,
I wonder how they could do so!
With a ring a ting tang,
And a ring a ting tang,
Poor old Robinson Crusoe!

Jack Sprat

Jack Sprat could eat no fat,
His wife could eat no lean,
And so between the two of them
They licked the platter clean.

Rub-a-Dub Dub

Rub-a-dub dub, three men in a tub,
And who do you think they be?
The butcher, the baker, the candle-stick maker,
Turn them out knaves all three.

Solomon Grundy

Solomon Grundy,
Born on Monday,
Christened on Tuesday,
Married on Wednesday,
Sick on Thursday,
Worse on Friday,
Died on Saturday,
Buried on Sunday,
That was the end
Of Solomon Grundy.

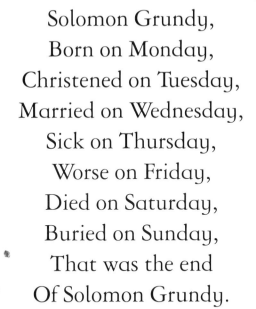

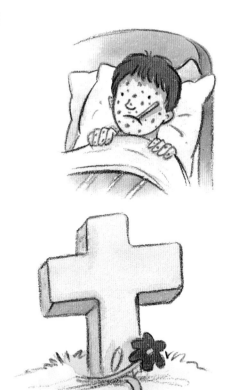

Me, Myself and I

Me, myself and I –
We went to the kitchen and ate a pie.
Then my mother she came in
And chased us out with a rolling pin.

Swan Swam Over the Sea

Swan swam over the sea –
Swim, swan, swim,
Swan swam back again,
Well swum swan.

Tent Trouble

Ross and Jane were on the swings in the campsite playground.

"This is great!" said Ross, pushing off as hard as he could.

Sam and Kim, who were staying in the tent next door to Ross and Jane, were watching Ross and Jane play.

"Swings are for babies," said Sam.

"It's fun," said Jane.

"We're going to have better fun," said Sam.

"What are you going to do?" asked Ross.

"We're not telling you," said Kim. And they ran off.

"I wonder what they're going to do?" said Jane.

"Let's follow them," said Ross.

Ross and Jane followed Sam and Kim across the campsite back to where their tents were pitched.

From behind the bushes, they watched Sam and Kim pulling out all the tent pegs in their parents' tent one by one

and laughing.

"Now this is fun!" Sam was saying to Kim.

"The tent is going to fall down!" said Jane to Ross.

"Look out!" shouted Ross, as loudly as he could.

Sam's mum and dad

looked out of the tent... just as it fell down around their ears with a huge flapping noise!

"Ouch!" cried Sam and Kim's dad, as a pole hit him on the head.

Sam and Kim's parents crawled out of the ruined tent.

"I wonder what happened?" said Sam and Kim's dad. "We must have not put it up properly."

Sam and Kim were trying hard not to giggle.

Ross stepped out from behind the bushes.

"It wasn't the wind," he said. "Sam and Kim pulled out all the tent pegs."

"They did," agreed Jane.

"Sam! Kim!" shouted their parents.

"It was a joke!" said Sam.

"I have a better joke," said their mum. She picked up the tent pegs and gave them to Sam and Kim.

"Put the tent back up!" she said.

The Royal Mystery

"Jed, go and tidy your room!" shouted Mum. She was in a really bad mood.

"But it is tidy!" Jed protested, stomping upstairs. "Maybe she's having trouble with a mission," he said to himself. "I'd better check what she's up to."

While Mum was in the shower, Jed took a look at her computer screen. Jed's mum was a spy for government agency Unit X. What she didn't know was that Jed sometimes helped out secretly with some of her missions.

"The Duchess of Muddleswick has been disappearing from her house every night," he read. "The government thinks she may be working as a spy. Your mission is to find out what she is doing."

Jed went back to his bedroom. He would follow Mum to work that evening.

Jed put a pillow under his duvet to make Elise the babysitter think he was asleep if she looked in on him. Then he turned out the light, opened his window and climbed out. He hid in the shadows, waiting for Mum to leave the house.

A few moments later, Mum came out and began to walk down the street. Jed followed her. After a bus ride and a long walk, she stopped outside a huge house.

"That must be the Duchess's mansion," Jed said to himself.

Mum's mobile phone rang. As she talked on the phone, she didn't notice a shadowy figure leave the house through a side door.

Jed watched. It was a woman wearing sunglasses – even though it was dark. Jed guessed it must be the Duchess.

One Dark Night

Paws tiptoed out into the dark farmyard. Mummy had told him to stay in the barn until he was old enough to go out at night, but he was impatient.

"*Toowhit, toowhoo!*" A loud hoot echoed through the trees, and a great dark shape swooped down and snatched something up.

"Just an owl," Paws told himself, creeping nervously on into the darkness. "Nothing to be afraid of!"

Strange rustlings came from every corner.

Grunt! Paws jumped. But it was just the old pig in the pigsty close by.

Then, all of a sudden, Paws froze in his tracks. Beneath the hen house two eyes glinted in the darkness. They came creeping towards him… this must be the fox Mummy had warned him about! But then, to his amazement, he saw it was Mummy!

"Back to the barn!" she said sternly. And Paws happily did as he was told. Maybe he would wait until he was older to go out at night, after all!

Naughty Duckling

Mummy Duck is in a flap.
"My naughty duckling won't come back!"

She's off to chase him, on his tail –
Following Little Duckling's trail.

"Go over the hill!" the little foal neighs,
"I saw Little Duckling run that way!"

"Along the fence!" baby calf moos,
"You'll catch him if you hurry, too!"

The piglets oink, "We saw him slide!
Up on the roof and down the side!"

"Look under here!" the lambs all baa,
"He can't have gone so very far!"

"He came past here!" cheeps little chick,
"He said hello, then ran off, quick!"

And there he is! He loves to roam.
But most of all he loves his home!

The White Feather

Duck was waddling around the farmyard when she saw a large white feather floating in the pond. She fished it out with her beak, and put it in her tail.

But when Pig saw Duck, he burst out laughing. "You look so silly!" he cried, rolling round in the mud.

"I thought I looked pretty," said Duck, feeling a bit sad.

Duck went to find Horse. "Do I look silly with my nice new feather?" she asked him.

"I think you look wonderful!" said Horse, kindly. "But that feather isn't yours. It belongs to Chicken."

"Then I'll give it back at once," said Duck. She went straight to see Chicken. "I've got your feather," said Duck. "I'm so sorry."

"Thank you!" cried Chicken, putting the feather back in her own tail, where it looked just perfect.

"And how beautiful you look with your fine yellow feathers, Duck," she said.

Duck waddled out into the farmyard feeling very pretty indeed!

Lost Bananas

One day, Elephant was stomping through the jungle when she found a huge bunch of bananas lying under a tree. "Someone must have lost these," she thought. "I'll go and ask Snake."

Elephant found Snake sunbathing on a rock. "Have you lost these bananas, Snake?" asked Elephant.

"How delicioussssss! But they're not my bananassss!" hissed Snake, and slithered into the trees.

"I'll just leave them here, then," said Elephant. "Someone will find them." And she plodded back into the jungle.

A giraffe with a long, thin neck came swaying past, and spotted the bananas sitting on the rock.

"What a pity! Someone has lost their dinner," she said, bending down to eat the thick jungle grass.

"Someone must want those bananas!" said Parrot, watching from a tree.

Suddenly she heard a rustling in the branches…

… and lots of monkeys came swinging through the trees!

"Of course! Monkeys love eating bananas!" cried Parrot.

"Wow, what a fantastic bunch of bananas!" said the monkeys. "Let's have a *huge* jungle feast! Come on everybody! Let's eat!"

There Was an Old Lady

There was an old lady
Who lived down our street,
You wouldn't believe all
The things she could eat.

For breakfast each morning,
A full slap up meal
Of nuts and bolts served in
A bicycle wheel!

She always took care
To never miss lunch,
On brooms, mops and buckets
She'd nibble and crunch.

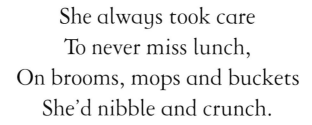

Trumpets and trombones were
Her favourite dinner,
But though always eating
She kept getting thinner.

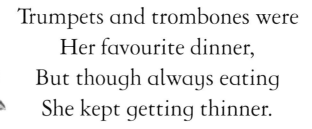

Finally, for supper she'd snack on
Some bees in their hives,
All swiftly washed down with
The forks, spoons and knives!

Did You Ever See...

Did you ever see a jester juggling with ice creams,
Or a pair of giant hamsters, wrestling in your dreams?
If you've never seen a crocodile swallow twenty conkers,
Then you, my friend, are honestly quite bonkers!

Did you ever see a puppy dancing with a brolly,
Or a pair of sweet old ladies pushing bandits on a trolley?
If you've never seen an elephant sitting on a daisy,
Then you, my friend, are honestly quite crazy!

Did you ever see a singing worm climbing up a wall,
Or a judge stand up in court, and catch a cricket ball?
If you've never seen a kangaroo asleep in silk pyjamas,
Then you, my friend, are honestly quite bananas!

I know people think I'm mad – but here's my explanation:
I make up lots of stuff with my wild imagination!

Treasure Map

Pirate captain Jenny and her band of ruthless pirates were very excited. They were on the hunt for treasure!

Captain Jenny showed them all the treasure map. There was an 'X' marked on it. It was six steps from a rock.

"There'll be gold doubloons and silver sovereigns, rubies red as blood, sapphires bluer than the sky and diamonds worth more than this entire ship!" she said.

Billy the cabin boy was as excited as everyone else. "I'd really like a gold doubloon," he thought. "Just one." But he didn't think that he'd be allowed any of the treasure. He was too young.

The pirates landed on the beach. "Come on, me hearties!" cried Jenny, jumping off the ship into the shallows with a big splash.

On the beach there was a big rock, just as the treasure map had promised.

Captain Jenny took six steps to the left. "One, two, three, four, five, six."

"Here we go!" she cried.

"Hooray!" cheered the pirates. They started to dig a hole with their shovels in the hot sun. Soon everyone was sweating. They dug and dug and dug – but there was no treasure.

"Oh dear," said Captain Jenny.

"No treasure!" said Bosun Bob.

"Maybe it's a fake map," said Crewman Charlie.

They were all fed up. Then Billy looked at the map again. "Er, Captain," he said.

"What, Billy?" said Captain Jenny.

"I think the map might be upside down," said Billy.

Captain Jenny looked at the map again. "Do you know, Billy, I think you might be right!" she said.

Captain Jenny took six steps to the right of the rock. "One, two, three, four, five, six."

The pirates dug a new hole.

"Treasure!" they all cried.

"Thanks to Billy," said Captain Jenny. "And as a reward, Billy, you can have a dozen gold doubloons!"

Car Wash

Eddie's dad was washing his car.

"I really hate this job!" he said to Eddie and Josh. "If you want to earn some money, you should wash people's cars."

Eddie and Josh thought this was a great idea. They made a big sign, filled some buckets with soapy water and borrowed some sponges.

Soon afterwards, Mr Cole drove in. "Hello, boys," he said. "I'll be your first customer!"

Eddie and Josh looked at the car. It was very muddy!

"This is going to take ages!" said Eddie.

Melinda, who lived down the road, was walking by.

"Hello, Melinda!" Eddie and Josh called.

"What are you doing?" asked Melinda. "That looks fun!"

Eddie had an idea. "It is fun!" he lied. "If you give us £1, you can help."

"Thank you!" said Melinda, looking pleased. "I haven't got the money, but I'll ask my dad for it later."

Eddie handed Melinda a sponge and did a high five with Josh behind her back.

Melinda was a hard worker, and soon the car was sparkling.

"You've done a great job, boys!" said Mr Cole. "Thank you."

Melinda's dad was the next person to pull into the drive.

"Hello, Dad!" said Melinda. "Can we wash your car?"

Eddie pointed to the sign. "It'll cost £1," he said. Melinda's dad got out his wallet.

"Please may I have £1 too, Dad?" asked Melinda. "I need to pay Eddie and Josh for letting me help."

Her dad put the wallet back in his pocket. "You'll do nothing of the sort!" he replied, crossly.

He turned to Eddie and Josh. "I'm going to speak to your parents!" he said.

Eddie and Josh's parents were not happy! "You two can wash Melinda's dad's car for free," said Josh's mum.

"Then you can wash our car for free," added Eddie's mum.

Eddie and Josh sighed.

"Can I help for free?" asked Melinda. "I love washing cars!"

Goodnight Kiss

"It's bedtime now, Oakey," said Mum.

Oakey curled up in the chair. His ears began to droop and he muttered, "Oh, that's not fair!"

"Have a drink first," smiled Mum, "then you must go."

Oakey's ears drooped and off he went. But he was back in a flash!

"Where's your drink?" asked Mum. "You haven't been very long. You look scared, Oakey. Is there something wrong?"

"There's a ghost in the hallway, hovering about. Look, there it is floating just above the ground," he wailed.

"Oh, Oakey, you've made a mistake. That's no ghost. It's just an old coat, hanging on the hook!" laughed Mum.

Oakey's ears drooped and off he went. But he was back in a flash!

"Why aren't you in bed, Oakey?" asked Mum.

"There's a great big lump beneath the sheets. I'm scared it's going to pounce. Please come and see," sniffed Oakey.

"Oh, Oakey, you've made a mistake. The only thing

underneath the sheets is your old teddy bear," smiled Mum.

Oakey's ears drooped and he got into bed. But he didn't close his eyes.

"Why aren't you asleep?" asked Mum.

"There are huge creepy crawlies underneath my bed," complained Oakey.

"They're just your slippers, Oakey. They won't be creeping anywhere without your feet inside," grinned Mum.

"That's it now, Oakey. Time to say goodnight." Mum turned and left the room, switching off the light.

Oakey lay in the dark for a little while. And then he saw it, standing by the door. The monster!

It moved across the floor and walked straight towards him.

The monster leaned over him and Oakey closed his eyes. What happened next gave Oakey an enormous surprise.

The monster picked him up and cuddled him tight.

Monsters just don't do that. This couldn't be right!

Then Mum's voice whispered, "Don't worry, it's just me. When I said 'Good night' just now, I forgot to give you this."

Then Monster Mum gave Oakey a goodnight kiss!

King of the Castle

Ross and Jane were exploring an old castle near the campsite they were staying on. They saw someone they knew.

"Oh no, it's Sam," said Ross. Sam was climbing a wall.

Jane pointed to the big sign. It said *Danger*!

"Come down!" said Jane.

"You will fall!" said Ross. But Sam carried on climbing. He stood on top of the wall. He marched up and down. "I'm the king of the castle!" he said.

"Look!" said Ross. "The wall is falling down."

"Sam, you are in danger!" said Jane.

Bang! A few bricks fell off the top of the wall.

"Watch out, Sam!" cried Jane.

"Don't be such a scaredy-cat!" shouted Sam, scornfully.

Crash! A whole section of the wall fell down. Sam slipped...

"*Sam!*" shouted Ross.

Sam just managed to hold on to the top of the wall with his fingertips. "Help me!" he shouted. "Help me! I'm about to fall!"

"Hold on!" said Ross.

Ross and Jane ran back to the campsite to get help.

Soon a fire engine arrived. The firemen put a ladder against the wall and lifted Sam down.

"Thank goodness you're safe," said Sam's mum, giving him a big hug.

"Don't do that again," said the fireman, sternly.

"I won't," said Sam. "Thank you for saving me."

And for once it looked as though Sam might mean it!

Witches on the Run

At night, when it's all dark and scary,
I peek from my covers, quite wary.
And there on the wall
Are shadows so tall –
Pointed hats, capes and noses all hairy.

They love casting spells late at night,
Their cauldron glows with a strange light.
It bubbles and spits,
Spilling slimy green bits,
And gives me and Teddy a fright!

My mum says that I must be dreaming,
When I spy witches high on the ceiling.
But they keep me awake
With the noise that they make,
All that ear-piercing cackling and screaming!

But tonight when they come I'll be ready,
All I need is to keep my aim steady.
One squirt from my gun,
Will have them on the run,
Witches hate getting wet, don't they, Teddy?

Meet-on-the-Road

"Now, pray, where are you going?" said Meet-on-the-Road.
"To school, sir, to school, sir," said Child-as-it-Stood.
"What have you in your basket, child?" said Meet-on-the-Road.
"My dinner, sir, my dinner, sir," said Child-as-it-Stood.

"What have you for dinner, child?" said Meet-on-the-Road.
"Some pudding, sir, some pudding, sir," said Child-as-it-Stood.
"Oh then, I pray, give me a share," said Meet-on-the-Road.
"I've little enough for myself, sir," said Child-as-it-Stood.

"What have you got that cloak on for?" said Meet-on-the-Road.
"To keep the wind and cold from me," said Child-as-it-Stood.
"I wish the wind would blow through you," said Meet-on-the-Road.
"Oh, what a wish! What a wish!" said Child-as-it-Stood.

"Pray, what are those bells ringing for?" said Meet-on-the-Road.
"To ring bad spirits home again," said Child-as-it-Stood.
"Oh, then I must be going, child!" said Meet-on-the-Road.
"So fare you well, so fare you well," said Child-as-it-Stood.

Sports Day

It was Sports Day at school. First there was the running race. All the animals lined up.

"On your marks, get set, GO!" said Mrs Beak, the teacher. Jed Giraffe had long legs. He won the running race.

Next was a beanbag race. Lucy Lion kept her head very still. She won the beanbag race.

Then there was a hopping race. Mikey Monkey won the hopping race.

But poor Helga Hippo didn't win a single race.

That playtime Helga sat on her own, feeling sorry for herself. "I'm no good at anything," she thought.

Then she heard loud shouts from the pond. Mikey had slipped in!

"Help!" he called. "I can't swim!"

"I can't swim, either!" said Jed.

"I can't swim either!" said Lucy.

"Help!" cried Mikey, desperately.

Helga could swim. She jumped in and saved Mikey. "I might not be a fast runner, a good beanbag balancer or a great hopper," she said. "But I can swim!"

"Well done, Helga!" said Mrs Beak.

A Stormy Day

"Lunch time!"

It was time for the builders to eat. The builders went to their hut to drink tea and eat sandwiches.

Digger had a rest. Dumper had a rest. Dozer had a rest.

Then a storm cloud came over. The wind began to blow and the rain began to fall.

"*Meow*!" mewed the cat who lived on the building site.

"The cat will get wet," said Digger.

"Her kittens will get cold," said Dumper. The cat was afraid. She hid her kittens in Digger's scoop.

"Look!" said the builders, when they came back from their lunch. The cat and her kittens were fast asleep curled up in Digger's scoop.

The builders took the cat and the kittens to the hut to keep them safe and dry from the storm.

Sippity, Sippity Sup

Sippity sup, sippity sup,
Bread and milk from a china cup.
Bread and milk from a bright silver spoon
Made of a piece of the bright silver moon.
Sippity sup, sippity sup,
Sippity, sippity sup.

Hannah Bantry

Hannah Bantry,
In the pantry,
Gnawing on a mutton bone;
How she gnawed it,
How she clawed it,
When she found herself alone.

Old King Cole

Old King Cole was a merry old soul,
And a merry old soul was he;
He called for his pipe, and he called for his bowl,
And he called for his fiddlers three.

Little Blue Ben

Little Blue Ben, who lives in the glen,
Keeps a blue cat and one blue hen,
Which lays of blue eggs a score and ten;
Where shall I find the little Blue Ben?

Eeper Weeper

Eeper Weeper, chimney sweeper,
Married a wife and could not keep her.
Married another,
Did not love her,
Up the chimney he did shove her!

Dame Trot

Dame Trot and her cat
Sat down for a chat;
The dame sat on this side
And puss sat on that.
"Puss," says the dame,
"Can you catch a rat,
Or a mouse in the dark?"
"Purr," says the cat.

The Prime Minister's Secret

"I have to leave early today, Jed," said Mum, grabbing her keys. "See you later!"

As the front door slammed shut, Jed switched on the TV. He didn't have to leave for school just yet.

He flicked onto the news channel. "No one knows what is wrong with the Prime Minister," said a newsreader. "He hasn't been seen in public for over a week."

Jed yawned and then went into the study to get his schoolbag. As he passed the computer, he couldn't resist checking to see what Mum was up to today. Jed's mum was a spy.

There was a photo of a bald man on the screen. He looked oddly familiar.

"The Prime Minister's wig went missing last week," Jed read. He looked at the photo again and his eyes widened. The man in the photo was the Prime Minister, without his thick mop of grey hair. The Prime Minister wore a wig and no one knew!

Jed read on. "The Prime Minister's dog chewed up his spare wig, and a new wig cannot be made as the Prime Minister's wig-maker has broken his arm in a skiing accident. You must find the lost wig as quickly as possible, Agent Best."

Jed grinned. "I'll have to think of a good excuse for being late for school today," he said.

Half an hour later, Jed was standing at the back of Number 10 Downing Street, where the Prime Minister lived. He checked that no one was looking and then quickly climbed the wall and dropped into the garden. He sneaked up to the house, grinning when he saw that the back door had a dog flap.

Jed squeezed through it and found himself in a large kitchen.

"Is that you, Bruno?" said a woman's voice. The voice was coming towards the kitchen.

Jed quickly ducked behind some recycling bins.

"Woof!" A big, shaggy dog brushed past him.

"Time for breakfast, Bruno," said the woman.

Jed spotted a cupboard. "I'll wait in there while she feeds the dog," he thought, slipping inside.

It was a cleaning cupboard. As his eyes got used to the dark, Jed spotted something in the corner. "That's a strange mop," he thought.

He leaned down to take a closer look. It wasn't a mop at all.

"It's the missing wig!" Jed whispered. Someone had mistaken it for a mop head!

Jed shook the wig and coughed as a cloud of dust filled the cupboard.

When the kitchen was empty again, Jed crept out of the cupboard, clutching the wig.

He went off to find the Prime Minister's office. When he found the right door, Jed hung the scruffy wig onto the door handle.

Then Jed gave the door two short raps and hid behind a nearby chair.

The door opened. Jed heard a gasp – and then saw a hand snatch up the wig and slam the door shut again.

Jed smiled. "I guess it's time for school now," he said to himself.

That evening, Mum arrived home from work early, in a very good mood.

Jed was watching the news. "Look at the Prime Minister!" he said. "He sure is having a bad hair day!"

One, Two

One, two, whatever you do,
Start it well and carry it through.
Try, try, never say die,
Things will come right,
You know, by and by.

Old Bandy Legs

As I was going to sell my eggs,
I met a man with bandy legs;
Bandy legs and crooked toes,
I tripped up his heels and he fell on his nose.

I Do Not Like Thee

I do not like thee, Doctor Fell,
The reason why, I cannot tell;
But this I know, and know full well,
I do not like thee, Doctor Fell.

My Mummy's Maid

Dingty diddlety,
My mummy's maid,
She stole oranges,
I am afraid;
Some in her pocket,
Some in her sleeve,
She stole oranges,
I do believe.

Charlie Wag

Charlie Wag,
Charlie Wag,
Ate the pudding
And left the bag.

Sunshine

A sunshiny shower
Won't last half an hour.

Farmyard Chase

Mother Hen sat on her nest and shook out her soft, fluffy feathers. She had an egg to keep warm. She had been sitting there for hours.

"I'm hungry," thought Mother Hen. Suddenly, Mother Hen saw a patch of sunlight by the barn door. She had an idea. She rolled her egg carefully over into the sun and packed some hay round it. "That will keep you warm," she said to her egg. "I won't be long."

And off she went to find some corn.

Horse came trotting up to the barn. He was hungry, too. He saw the hay by the barn door.

"Yummy!" he neighed, as he pushed his smooth, velvety muzzle into the hay. Bump! Horse's nose nudged Mother Hen's egg.

The egg rocked, and then it rolled. It rolled across the yard.

"Oh no!" neighed Horse. He trotted after the egg as it tumbled towards a pile of apples under the apple tree.

Pig was snuffling around the apple tree as the egg rolled past his nose.

"Oh no!" squealed Pig. "Catch that egg before it cracks!" And he scampered after the egg as it tumbled into the grassy meadow.

Sheep was munching the tufty grass in the meadow as the egg rolled past her.

"Oh no!" bleated Sheep. "Catch that egg before it cracks!" And she skipped after the egg as it tumbled down the hill.

At the bottom of the hill, Cow was lying down, having a rest after lunch. Bump! The egg bounced against Cow's nose.

"Ouch!" mooed Cow. "What was that?" And she stared at the egg. Horse, Pig and Sheep came running down the hill.

"Catch that egg before it cracks!" they called.

"I have caught it," replied Cow.

"My egg!" clucked Hen, flapping her way down the hill.

Just then, there was a loud *Crack!*

"Someone must have cracked it!" clucked Hen. *Crack!* The crack got bigger still.

Suddenly, the egg cracked wide open. Out hopped a soft, fluffy ball of yellow feathers.

"It was me!" cheeped the little fluffy chick. "I cracked it all by myself!"

Fire! Fire!

Nee naw! Nee naw! the sirens say,
The big red fire engine is on its way.

Round the corner with a screech of tyres,
The fire engine races to put out fires.

Listen to the sirens! They seem to say,
"Coming through! Please make way!"

See the smoke! The barn fire grows!
Quickly! Quickly! Roll out the hose.

Here comes the water – swoosh! – from the spout.
Splish! Splash! Hiss! And the fire is out!

Choo! Choo!

All aboard, off we go!
The wheels are turning – start off slow!

Choo! Choo! Choo! Count with me,
Shiny carriages, one, two, three.

Up the hill, along the track,
Faster, faster, clickety-clack!

Across the bridge the train goes by,
Clouds of smoke puff way up high.

Here's the tunnel… Whoo! Whoo!
The whistle blows. We're coming through!

Chuffa! Chuffa! At last we're here!
"Hip hooray!" the passengers cheer.

The Fantastic Firework

Whoosh! A fountain of gold stars fell through the night sky. It was Bonfire Night in the village of Upper Redding and a big crowd had gathered to enjoy the spectacular fireworks display.

High above them, Ag the Alien was coming in to land in his brand-new supercharged spaceship.

"Ah, home again!" he said. Unfortunately, Ag wasn't anywhere near his home. He didn't know it, but he was horribly lost.

Down below, a boy called Mike tugged at his father's arm. "Hey! Look over there, Dad," he cried. "That rocket's coming down, not going up!"

Ag thought he had made a perfect landing. Then he looked through his skyscreen and gasped. He hastily pressed the *Where Am I?* switch, and a message flashed up: *Planet Earth.*

"Earth!" shrieked Ag. He realized that he must have activated the hyperthrust device by mistake and that he'd better press it again, quick, when something happened that stopped him in his tracks.

Two fountains blossomed across the sky in a brilliant flash of yellow.

Now, Ag loved fireworks. In fact, everyone did on his planet.

"Just think how thrilled everyone at home would be," Ag thought, "if I let off a new firework they'd never seen before." So Ag armed himself with a laser megablaster, jumped out of the spacecraft and hurried off towards the Upper Redding bonfire.

Bang! He ran straight into Mike, who had come to check out the strange rocket.

"Aagh!" yelled Mike.

"Pleased to meet you," said Ag, feeling very confused. He had been about to blow the odd-looking creature to smithereens. But it had known his name!

Looking at the megablaster, Mike quickly decided it would be wise to make friends, if that was what the alien wanted to do. "Er, pleased to meet you, too," he replied.

"Now," said Ag. "I need your fireworks."

"I know just what you want," said Mike, thinking quickly. "It's over there in that clump of trees, and it's the best thing in the show. But you'll need to beam it up, because it's so big."

Ag was delighted. He beamed the giant firework aboard and whooshed away, seconds before everyone started to gather for the grand finale. To Mike's surprise, they started clapping, as if the grand finale had already happened.

"What a fantastic firework!" Mike's dad said. "It looked just like a huge space rocket being launched!" Mike grinned to himself.

And meanwhile, on the other side of the galaxy, the letters of Upper Redding ignited in a blaze of golden fountains.

"Where did you get it?" Ag's friends exclaimed.

"Oh, just a little place I know," he grinned.

Monster Munch

I may be big and hairy
And I may look mean and tough,
But I'm a nice, kind monster,
And I've simply had enough!

It's really most distressing
When you scream and run away –
I have no plans to eat you,
All I want to do is play!

Oh, can't you see I'm lonely?
Can't you tell I'm feeling blue?
I've got no friends to talk to,
But I like the look of you!

I'm just about to make some lunch,
And I'd love it if you'd come.
You will? Oh, great, that's perfect!
Ha, ha – I tricked you! Yum!

London Bridge

London Bridge is falling down,
Falling down, falling down.
London Bridge is falling down,
My fair lady.

Build it up with iron bars,
Iron bars, iron bars,
Build it up with iron bars,
My fair lady.

Iron bars will bend and break,
Bend and break, bend and break,
Iron bars will bend and break,
My fair lady.

Build it up with stone so strong,
Stone so strong, stone so strong,
Huzza! 'twill last for ages long,
My fair lady.

Little Elephant's Clever Trick

Little Elephant set off for a walk. Today he wanted to explore. He hadn't gone far when he met Zebra.

Little Elephant had never seen a zebra before. He looked at Zebra's snazzy stripes. Then he looked at his own plain skin. Little Elephant was puzzled.

"Excuse me," Little Elephant said. "Why are you stripy?"

"So I can hide," replied Zebra. "When I'm in the grass, out on the plain, it's really hard to see me. I'll show you!"

He galloped off. Little Elephant tried to see where he went, but Zebra had disappeared.

Little Elephant was amazed. "You're right! It is hard to see you. That's so clever."

Little Elephant wandered on. Before long, Little Elephant met Giraffe. He had never seen a giraffe before.

Little Elephant looked at Giraffe's pretty patches. Then he looked at his own grey skin.

"Excuse me," Little Elephant said. "Why are you covered in patches?"

"So I can hide," Giraffe replied. "When I'm under the trees and the sun's shining, it's really hard to see me. I'll show you!"

Giraffe walked over to some trees. Little Elephant tried to see where she went, but Giraffe had disappeared. Little Elephant was impressed.

"You're right! It is hard to see you. That's so clever." And Little Elephant wandered on.

Little Elephant was starting to feel very sad. "I can't hide anywhere," he thought. "Everyone would be able to see me. I wish I was like Zebra or Giraffe."

He knelt down, bowed his head, and began to cry.

Giraffe and Zebra came back with Crocodile. "Where's Little Elephant?" asked Giraffe. "He was here a minute ago."

"Well, he's not here now," said Zebra. "There's just that old rock over there."

The rock began to giggle. "It's me!" called Little Elephant. "I'm not a rock!"

"What a clever trick!" smiled Zebra.

"You don't need grass or trees," laughed Giraffe.

"You can hide anywhere, just like that," added Zebra.

"So I can," said Little Elephant.

"We came to see if you'd like to play," said Little Elephant's new friends.

"Yes, please!" replied Little Elephant. "I'd like to play hide-and-seek."

285

The Grand Old Duke of York

The grand old Duke of York,
He had ten thousand men;
He marched them up to the top of the hill,
And he marched them down again!

And when they were up they were up,
And when they were down they were down;
And when they were only halfway up,
They were neither up nor down.

What Is the Rhyme for Porringer?

What is the rhyme for porringer?
The King he had a daughter fair,
And gave the Prince of Orange her.

Go to Bed

Go to bed late,
Stay very small;
Go to bed early
Grow very tall.

Grey Goose and Gander

Grey goose and gander,
Waft your wings together,
And carry the good king's daughter
Over the one strand river.

Ten Little Men

Ten little men standing straight,
Ten little men open the gate,
Ten little men all in a ring,
Ten little men bow to the king,
Ten little men dance all day,
Ten little men hide away.

I Met a Man

As I was going up the stair
I met a man who wasn't there.
He wasn't there again today –
Oh how I wish he'd go away!

Tickly Sheep

One morning, Farmer Fred was in the kitchen having his hair cut. Farmer Fred's wife Jenny was snipping away with the scissors.

"Hurry up," said Farmer Fred. "I've got to shear all the sheep today."

"Well, stop wriggling," laughed Jenny.

"But it tickles," chuckled Farmer Fred.

"I've never known anyone make such a fuss about having their hair cut," laughed Jenny, making the final snip.

Farmer Fred and Patch went up to Fern Hill to round up the sheep. Farmer Fred whistled a signal to Patch: Peep! Peeeep! Patch ran around the field, herding the sheep towards the yard.

Farmer Fred whistled a different signal: Peeeep! Peep! Patch soon had the sheep lined up outside the barn.

Inside the barn, Farmer Fred switched on his shears. Whizz, whizz, whizz went the shears.

"There's nothing quite like shearing sheep," he smiled, and began to sing.

One by one, Farmer Fred sheared the sheep. The woolly fleeces which came off the sheep collected on the barn floor. All went well until it was Shirley Sheep's turn.

Whizz, whizz, went the shears. As soon as the buzzing shears touched her side, Shirley began to wriggle and jiggle.

"Stop wriggling," cried Farmer Fred, as he tried to hold her still. He had forgotten just how ticklish Shirley was!

"Rumbling radishes!" Fred gasped, when he had finished. Shirley had wriggled about so much that she had big bald patches all over her woolly fleece. She looked very peculiar!

"Never fear, I've an idea!" cried Farmer Fred cheerfully. He dashed off to his workshop and disappeared inside.

Very soon, Farmer Fred came out of the workshop holding two old tyres tied onto some rope.

"This," Farmer Fred said grandly, "is my Super Sheep-defleecer!"

Farmer Fred helped Shirley Sheep to step through the tyres and slowly lifted her off the ground. He turned on the shears and tried again.

And although Shirley wriggled and giggled, Farmer Fred sheared off all her wool.

Farmer Fred let Shirley Sheep down and helped her from the tyres.

"Baa?" asked Shirley Sheep. She looked at the other animals. But they were all laughing so much at Shirley Sheep's stripy haircut they couldn't answer.

While Fred collected up the sheep fleeces, the animals gathered around Shirley Sheep.

"She can't possibly go around looking like that," said Hetty Hen. "Everyone will laugh at her."

"We have to do something," agreed Harry Horse. "Patch, what can we do?"

Suddenly Patch remembered Farmer Fred having his hair cut.

"Woof, woof!" he barked. "Leave it to me." Patch raced to the kitchen where Jenny had put the scissors, comb and mirror into a bowl.

"Woof, woof!" barked Patch, pushing the bowl outside just as Farmer Fred was crossing the yard.

"What's that, Patch?" laughed Fred. "I haven't got time to give you a hair cut now." Just then Shirley trotted up.

"Hold on!" said Farmer Fred. "I've had an even better idea!" He picked up the bowl and raced back to the barn.

Before long Shirley was sitting in her very own wool-cutting parlour.

"Now, would madam like a short and curly cut?" laughed Farmer Fred, as he began snipping away.

And this time, Shirley didn't giggle or wriggle until all that was left was a curly fringe.

"Perfect," said Farmer Fred, as he tied a huge blue ribbon in Shirley's lovely curls.

Shirley walked proudly around the farmyard. Everyone, including Jenny, gathered around to admire her.

They all agreed that she was the prettiest sheep on the farm.

"I've never known anyone make such a fuss about having their hair cut," said Farmer Fred. Jenny looked at Patch and laughed.

Garden Makeover

Josh's mum was doing some gardening. It gave Josh an idea.

He hurried round to Eddie's. "Let's see if anyone will pay us to do some gardening," he suggested.

Mr Peacock across the road was happy to be asked. "I'll pay you to mow the grass and do some weeding," he said. "The lawn mower is in the shed."

"My turn first!" said Eddie, starting up the engine.

It wasn't easy to steer the mower in a straight line. "Oops!" Eddie muttered, as he ploughed through a flowerbed.

Josh began to pull up weeds. "Oops!" he said, as each weed turned out to be a carrot.

Mr Peacock came hurrying down the garden path. "My beautiful flowers!" he cried. "And my prize carrots!"

"We're sorry, Mr Peacock," said Josh.

"We're not very good at gardening," Eddie added.

With a sigh, Mr Peacock bent down to inspect the damage

to his carrots. He picked up something shiny from the earth.

"What's this?" he asked. And then he gasped. "It's a Roman coin!" he said. "Quick lads, get digging – see if you can find any more!"

Together, Josh, Eddie and Mr Peacock dug up a whole mound of Roman coins. "My mum runs the shop at the local museum," said Eddie. "She says that the curator there knows all there is to know about the Romans."

"Let's take them down there!" said Mr Peacock.

The museum curator was very excited when she saw the coins. "These are very rare!" she said. "They might prove that there were once Romans living around here."

She looked at Mr Peacock. "And they're probably very valuable!"

Back home, Mr Peacock paid Josh and Eddie.

"I think you've given us too much money, Mr Peacock," said Eddie.

"No I haven't," he said. "It's to say thank you for helping me find the coins." Then he winked at them. "Now I'll be able to afford a proper gardener!"

Washing Up

When I was a little boy
I washed my mummy's dishes;
I put my finger in one eye,
And pulled out golden fishes.

What's the News?

"What's the news of the day,
Good neighbour, I pray?"
"They say the balloon
Is gone up to the moon."

The Queen of Hearts

The Queen of Hearts, she made some tarts,
All on a summer's day;
The Knave of Hearts, he stole the tarts,
And took them clean away.
The King of Hearts called for the tarts,
And beat the Knave full sore;
The Knave of Hearts brought back the tarts,
And vowed he'd steal no more.

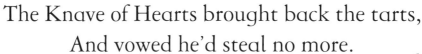

King Arthur

When famed King Arthur ruled this land
He was a goodly king:
He took three pecks of barley meal
To make a bag pudding.
A rare pudding the king did make,
And stuffed it well with plums;
And in it put such lumps of fat,
As big as my two thumbs.
The king and queen did eat thereof,
And noblemen beside,
And what they could not eat that night
The queen next morning fried.

Cobbler, Cobbler

Cobbler, cobbler, mend my shoe,
Get it done by half past two;
Stitch it up, and stitch it down,
Then I'll give you half a crown.

Rain

Rain before seven,
Fine by eleven.

I Just Can't Sleep

It's time to sleep.
I've brushed my teeth
And read my book,
I've put my bathrobe
On the hook, and...
I just can't sleep.
The bed's too hot,
The light's too bright,
There are far too many
Sounds tonight, and...
Maybe I'll sleep.
I think I might,
I think I'll – yawn –
Turn out the light.
Good night.
Zzzzzz...

Holiday Time

We're off on holiday. Oh, what fun!
There may be rain or there may be sun.
But we'll all have a lovely time together,
And enjoy ourselves, whatever the weather!

Bunny in a Hurry

Tick tock! It's eight o'clock!
Can you tell the time?
Wake up, Bunny! Don't be late!
It's time to rise and shine.

Tick tock! It's twelve o'clock!
No time for any stops!
Bunny has a bouncy lunch,
Munching as he hops!

Tick tock! It's three o'clock!
So many things to do,
Like finding everything he needs
To make a carrot stew.

Tick tock! It's six o'clock!
And something smells delicious!
Hurry, Bunny, eat your stew!
You've got to wash the dishes!

Tick tock! It's seven o'clock!
Shhhh! Don't make a peep.
What a busy day it's been.
Now Bunny's fast asleep!

Jungle Hide-and-seek

Crouching in the jungle,
Roaring by a tree,
Looking for his dinner,
Who can you see?

Deep in the jungle,
Hiding up a tree,
Eating a big banana,
Who can it be?

Down beside the river,
Showing lots of teeth,
Waiting still and silent,
Who's underneath?

High up in the branches,
Noisy as can be,
With bright, shiny feathers,
Who's in the tree?

Creeping through the jungle,
Such a king is he,
Fierce, gold and furry,
Who can it be?

The Mountain Mission

Jed was helping Elise the babysitter prepare dinner when Mum arrived home. She came into the kitchen, and put two plane tickets onto the table.

"Surprise! We're flying to Switzerland first thing tomorrow," she said. "So we'd better start packing!"

"Are we going skiing?" asked Jed excitedly.

"Yes, we're staying in a luxury ski resort," replied Mum.

"Wow!" said Elise. "I wish I was coming!"

Jed was curious. Why had his mum suddenly decided to take this holiday? It must have something to do with her work as a spy, he guessed.

While Mum was packing, Jed sneaked upstairs, turned on her computer and checked her emails.

He soon found out why they were really going. Some plans for a new spy plane had been stolen and Mum's mission was to get them back. An enemy agent called Max Blatt had the plans in his Swiss mountain hideout.

"This could be

Mum's most dangerous mission yet," Jed said to himself. "Good job I'm going along too."

"Wow!" said Jed, as they arrived in the ski resort. He almost forgot why they were really there as he looked up at the snow-covered mountains. He couldn't wait to get out on those ski runs. He loved skiing.

Mum was looking up, too. Jed followed her gaze. She was staring at a building at the top of a nearby mountain.

"That must be Blatt's hideout," Jed guessed. It was a long way up. Jed knew that his mum wasn't very good at skiing. She'd never make it all the way down that mountain. "I must act fast, before Mum tries anything stupid," he said to himself.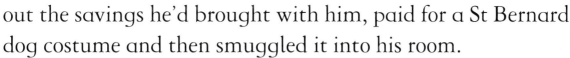

While Mum was unpacking, Jed went to explore the resort. Spotting a shop that sold fancy dress costumes, he had an idea. He took out the savings he'd brought with him, paid for a St Bernard dog costume and then smuggled it into his room.

"At least this silly disguise will keep me warm in the snow!" Jed thought as he put on the furry outfit the following morning.

There was only one way up the mountain, in the ski lift. Some skiers laughed when Jed got in.

"I didn't know dogs could ski!" one of them joked. At the top

of the mountain, Jed left the skiers behind. He made his way to the security fence surrounding Blatt's hideout and climbed over it.

Sneaking in through an open window, Jed found Blatt's office and began to look around for the plans. "They must be in here somewhere," he thought.

Suddenly three large dogs appeared. Jed was about to run when he saw that they didn't look at all fierce. They wanted to make friends.

"My costume must have fooled them," Jed thought with a relieved grin.

He found the plans, grabbed them and ran to the back door, almost tripping over a dog basket. "That will come in handy!" he said, picking it up. It was great fun sledging

down the mountain in the basket.

Soon Jed was back in his hotel. He went up to the reception desk.

"Will you send these papers up to Frances Best in Room 303, please?" he asked, handing over the plans.

"Mum will love the room service in this hotel!" Jed chuckled to himself.

My Hobby Horse

I had a little hobby horse, it was well shod,
It carried me to London, niddety nod,
And when we got to London we heard a great shout,
Down fell my hobby horse and I cried out:
"Up again, hobby horse, if thou be a beast,
When we get to our town we will have a feast,
And if there be but a little, why thou shall have some,
And dance to the bag-pipes and beating of the drum."

Engine, Engine

Engine, engine, number nine,
Sliding down Chicago line;
When she's polished she will shine,
Engine, engine, number nine.

Red Sky

Red sky at night,
Shepherd's delight;
Red sky in the morning,
Shepherd's warning.

Robin Hood

Robin Hood has gone to the wood;
He'll come back again if we are good.

There Was a Little Boy

There was a little boy and a little girl
Lived in an alley;
Says the little boy to the little girl,
"Shall I, oh, shall I?"
Says the little girl to the little boy,
"What shall we do?"
Says the little boy to the little girl,
"I will kiss you."

And That's All

There was an old man,
And he had a calf,
And that's half;
He took him out of the stall,
And put him on the wall,
And that's all.

Lost and Found

It was Show and Tell time in Class 2B.

Sam and Jed showed their new Perry Hill football shirts.

"Who else is a Perry Hill fan?" asked Miss Bell.

Joe put up his hand. So did Clare, the new girl in class.

Joe sighed. He really wanted to go and see Perry Hill play that Saturday, but it cost five pounds and he didn't have any pocket money left.

That break, Joe was kicking a ball around on his own when he saw something fluttering by. Joe leapt and grabbed it. It was a five pound note. He put the money in his pocket. Result!

After break, though, Clare was very upset.

"I've lost five pounds," she said to Miss Bell.

Joe thought about it.

He knew that the money was Clare's. Deep down, he had known all along that it wasn't his.

"I found it," said Joe.

"Thank you!" said Clare.

"Well done, Joe!" said Miss Bell.

The next day after school, Joe

spotted Jared Jones at the school gate. He was the top striker at Perry Hill football club.

"Look!" said Joe to Sam and Jed. "Jared Jones! I wonder what he's doing here?"

"He's talking to Clare!" said Sam.

"Why isn't he talking to us?" said Jed. "We're much better at football than she is."

Then Clare called across the playground, "Over here, Joe!"

Joe went across the playground towards Jared. He felt a bit nervous about meeting him. Jared was such an amazing footballer! Joe really hoped that one day he would be as good as Jared was.

"Jared is my big brother," Clare told Joe.

"Wow!" said Joe.

"Thanks for helping my sister," said Jared, handing Joe a ticket. Joe looked. It was three tickets to Saturday's match, in the best seats in the stadium.

"See you at the match on Saturday," said Jared. "And I hope you and your friends can come and meet the rest of the Perry Hill team after the match as well."

"Thanks!" said Joe.

Vicky the Very Silly Vet

"Good morning!" called Vet Vicky as she opened the door to her surgery. "How are all my animals today?"

She lined up the breakfast bowls and animal feed on the table and began to put out the food. Then... DING! went the doorbell.

"Oh!" cried Vicky. " My first patient is here already!" As quickly as she could, she put the bowls in the cages — but didn't look to see who was getting what! Patch the puppy got the bird seed, Hickory and Dickory the mice got the dog food, Percy the Parrot got the cat food and Tabby got the mice's sunflower seeds! What's more, Vicky had left all the cage doors wide open.

Fortunately, this had happened before and the animals knew just what to do. Hickory and Dickory found their sunflower seeds in Tabby's basket, Tabby discovered her cat food in Percy's cage, Percy pecked at his bird seed in Patch's cage, and Patch found his dog food in the mouse cage.

"Come in," said Vicky to her first patient. Then a thought crossed her mind. Hadn't she left the cage doors open? She gulped. What dreadful mess would there be?

But the clever animals were all back in their own cages. Vicky saw the clean and tidy room and grinned. "Treats for tea!" she whispered.

Barmy Builder Benny

One morning, Benny the builder arrived at Polly the postlady's house.

"I want you to build a Wendy house for my grandchildren," she said. "It should have two doors, five windows, and a sloping roof."

Polly left for the post office, and Benny went out to start work. He tried to remember everything that Polly had said, but he got confused. Was it five windows and two doors? Or two windows and five doors? Was the roof flat or sloping? Benny decided he would just have to do the best he could.

When Polly got home from work what a surprise she had! The Wendy house's roof was flat. There were five doors on one side of the house, and two windows on another side.

"It's all wrong!" said Polly. "How will you fix it in time?"

Benny didn't have a chance to answer, because just then Polly's five grandchildren arrived.

"Look! A Wendy house!" they cried. "There's a door for each of us! And we can climb on the roof! Thank you, Granny!"

"Well, I think you should thank Benny," said Polly, smiling.

Benny smiled too. "I just did my best," he said.

Fearless Fireman Fred

Fred hurried into the fire station with a bag of nice plump sausages. It was his turn to cook lunch for the firemen on the shift.

"Ooops!" he said, as he bumped into Benny the builder, who had come to repair the door.

Suddenly the alarm bell rang.

"Emergency!" cried the firemen, sliding down the pole and into their fire-fighting gear.

"What about the sausages?" cried Fred.

"I'll look after them for you!" called Benny.

The emergency was in Tony's Pizza Parlour – one of the pizza ovens had caught fire!

"We'll have that blaze out in a jiffy," said Fred.

"Thank you!" said Tony, as the firemen took their equipment back to the truck. "I can get back to baking pizzas now!"

"Look!" said Fred. "Smoke up ahead!"

NEE-NAW! went the siren as the engine raced to the scene of the fire. The smoke was coming from the fire station!

"Sorry, fellows," said Benny, running out. "I burnt the sausages."

Fortunately, Fred had an idea.

"Don't worry, guys," he said. "A yummy extra-large pizza will be a perfect lunch for all of us!"

Potty Polly Postlady

"Good morning, Polly!" said Mr Price the postmaster. "Your postbag is all ready – and it looks extra-full today!"

Polly tore around the corner of Jackson Road on her bicycle. But her bike started to get slower and slower. She realized she had a puncture.

"Oh no!" said Polly. "I'll have to walk my round today!"

Polly rushed and hurried, but by eleven o'clock her postbag was still half full. Then suddenly she saw something that gave her a brilliant idea.

"Jack, may I borrow your skateboard, please?" Polly asked.

Polly had never been on a skateboard before. She wibbled and wobbled… then WHOOSHED down the street.

Polly finished her round at lightning speed. "This is quicker than walking," she said, "and much more fun than my bike!"

At five to twelve Polly staggered through the door of the post office. "I'm back, Mr Price," she gasped.

"Well done, Polly!" said Mr Price. "Benny the builder brought back your bike. We'll have to mend that puncture right away."

"Oh, there's no hurry, Mr Price," said Polly. "I've found a much better form of transport for a potty postlady like me!"

The Queen's Pudding

Jim was the youngest, smallest and most hard-worked kitchen boy in the kitchens of the Queen of Hungerbert.

People shouted at him all day long: "Take this to the Queen!" "The Princess needs this now!" "Quickly!" "Move!"

One day the cook shouted at Jim, as usual.

"Take this pudding to the Queen! Now!" she said, giving Jim a dish of bananas and custard.

Jim took it to the Queen. The Queen took a bite.

"I like banana," she said. "But I don't like custard."

Jim went back to the kitchen.

Cook made jelly and ice cream. Jim took it to the Queen.

The Queen took a bite. "I like ice cream," she said. "But I don't like the jelly."

Cook made apple pie and cream.

"I like cream," said the Queen. "But I don't like pie."

"Oh dear!" said Cook. "The Queen only likes banana, ice cream and cream."

"That makes a banana split!" said Jim.

"You might just be right, Jim," said Cook. She made a banana split.

Jim took it to the Queen. She took a bite.

"I love it!" she said.

Jim went back to the kitchen and told Cook.

"Well done, Jim!" said Cook.

Mikey Is Busy

It was quiet time at school. All the animals were busy. All except Mikey Monkey. Mikey didn't like quiet time. He liked noisy-running-around-and-swinging-from-trees time.

Lucy Lion was deep in a book. Mikey tip-toed up and closed the covers with a snap.

"Go away, Mikey," said Lucy. "You've made me lose my place!"

Helga Hippo was painting a picture of some flowers. Mikey tipped over the paint. Red paint went all over the floor.

"Mikey!" said Helga.

Jed was building a block tower. It was almost twenty bricks high! Then Mikey deliberately bumped into the blocks...

"Mikey!" cried Jed. "That was my tallest tower ever."

Then Mikey stood on one of the school chairs. He balanced on one foot, then on the other foot. He leant backwards...

Crash! The chair fell over onto the ground.

Mrs Beak the teacher looked up from her desk.

"Are you busy, Mikey?" she said.

"No," said Mikey.

"This mess you've made will keep you busy then, Mikey!" said Mrs Beak. "Tidy up!"

For Sale

Jamie and Kay got out of the removal van and looked at their new house. The 'For Sale' sign was still up outside it.

"I don't like it," said Kay.

"Our old house was much better," said Jamie.

Mum and Dad didn't say anything, but Kay and Jamie could tell that they were thinking the same thing.

Inside, all the rooms were empty. The sound of the family's footsteps echoed.

"It doesn't feel like home," said Jamie. Then he heard a funny noise coming from the next room.

"*Mew! Mew! Mew!*"

Jamie ran next door. In a corner of the room was a cat and her three kittens.

"Look, Mum!" cried Jamie.

"She must have sneaked in while the house was empty," said Mum. "We can't throw them out. It was their home before it was ours!"

Kay stroked the cat. Jamie gently stroked one of the kittens.

"Now it feels like home," Jamie said.

Funfair Thief

Ross and Jane were at the funfair near their holiday campsite.

"What shall we go on first?" said Jane.

"The Big Wheel!" said Ross. They climbed into the swinging chairs and carefully fastened their safety belts.

And they were off! The wheel turned. Ross and Jane rose up... up... up... into the air. They could see all the funfair.

"There's Sam and Kim!" said Jane. Sam and Kim, who were staying in the tent next to them, were at the coconut stall.

The wheel went round and round. Then it started to slow down. The ride was nearly over.

Then Ross grabbed Jane's arm. "Look down there!" he said. A man was stealing a handbag!

"Stop that thief!" they shouted.

As soon as the Big Wheel stopped, Jane and Ross jumped off.

"Look, there he is!" said Jane.

"Stop that thief!" shouted Ross, sprinting after him.

They chased the thief past the candy-floss stall, past the Helter-Skelter, past Danny's Daring Dodgems and past the Marvellous Merry-go-round.

"Ouch!" said a man, as Ross bumped right into him.

"Sorry!" gasped Ross.

The thief ran past the coconut stall towards the exit.

"Sam!" called Ross. "Stop that thief!"

Four coconuts rolled out in front of the thief. His legs slid out from under him.

"Aaaargh!"

He fell to the ground.

"That stopped you!" said Sam.

"Well done, Sam!" said Jane.

"That was fun!" laughed Kim.

The thief was led away by the police. "You've got some questions to answer, young man," the policeman said.

"Thank you!" said the handbag's owner.

"You can all have free funfair rides for the day," said the fairground owner. "Anything you like. And you can have as much free food as you can eat."

"Great!" said the four friends, smiling.

Warning

The robin and the redbreast,
The robin and the wren:
If you take them from their nest
You'll never thrive again.

The Little, Rusty, Dusty Miller

Oh the little, rusty, dusty miller,
Dusty was his coat,
Dusty was his colour,
Dusty was the kiss
I got from the miller.
If I had my pockets
Full of gold and silver,
I would give it all
To my dusty miller.

Mr East's Feast

Mr East gave a feast;
Mr North laid the cloth;
Mr West did his best;
Mr South burnt his mouth
With eating a hot potato.

Catch Him

Catch him, crow! Carry him, kite!
Take him away till the apples are ripe;
When they are ripe and ready to fall,
Here comes a baby, apples and all.

Wine and Cakes

Wine and cakes for gentlemen,
Hay and corn for horses,
A cup of ale for good old wives,
And kisses for the lasses.

Wee Willie Winkie

Wee Willie Winkie runs through the town,
Upstairs and downstairs in his nightgown,
Peeping through the keyhole, crying through the lock,
"Are the children in their beds? It's past eight o'clock!"

Try It, You'll Like It!

It was the last day of school before the winter holidays and Sophie and Daniel were really excited.

"We're taking snowboarding lessons over the holiday," Sophie told all their classmates.

"Me too," said Jason.

"What have you got planned, Amir?" Daniel asked.

"Let me guess," Jason interrupted. "Playing computer games – right, Amir?"

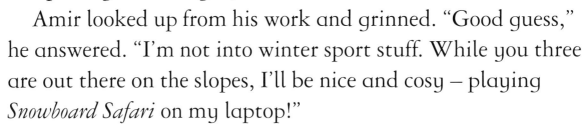

Amir looked up from his work and grinned. "Good guess," he answered. "I'm not into winter sport stuff. While you three are out there on the slopes, I'll be nice and cosy – playing *Snowboard Safari* on my laptop!"

Ten days later, it was time for the first snowboarding lesson. Daniel and Sophie pulled on their goggles, hats and gloves, and then grabbed their boards and clumped outside. A small group was gathered nearby, and a man with a clipboard called out names.

"Daniel and Sophie Lutz?"

"Here!" Daniel and Sophie said.

"Jason Walker?"

"Here!" Jason called back.

"Amir Mahmood?"

Daniel and Sophie looked at each other in surprise.

"Amir Mahmood?" the instructor called again.

"I'm here," he said, standing next to the twins.

"I thought you didn't like winter sports," Daniel whispered.

"I don't," Amir whispered back, grumpily. "My parents didn't want me to spend the holiday in front of the computer so they gave me boarding lessons as a surprise."

The class spent the next thirty minutes in one spot. They learned how to stand, balance and lean on the snowboard.

"Ready to try the real thing?" the instructor asked.

"Yes!" shouted most of the group.

"Not really," muttered Amir.

They followed the instructor to the drag lift that would carry each of them to the top of the beginners' slope.

"Sophie, you first," the instructor said. "Just grab the cable, lean back a little and let it pull you up the hill."

At the top, Daniel and Sophie stood with Amir and Jason.

"Ready?" Daniel said.

"It looks steep," Amir replied.

Sophie pointed her board sideways and bent her knees. Daniel and Jason did the same. Amir just watched.

"Let's go!" Sophie said.

She slid a few metres and then fell backwards into the snow.

Jason raced past her. "I'm going too fast!" he yelled. He swerved and tumbled into a snow bank.

"Not any more!" Sophie called.

Daniel laughed and then turned to Amir. "Our turn next!" he said.

But Amir shook his head. "In a minute," he replied.

Daniel pushed off to catch up with Sophie. Together, they slipped, stumbled and rolled down the hill.

"Let's go again!" Sophie said at the bottom. When they got to the top, Amir was still waiting.

"Come on, Amir," Sophie said. "We're all hopeless!"

Amir gave a wobbly smile. He took a step forward. "I guess if you can fall down the hill, I can too." He pointed his board, bent his knees and started to slide forwards.

"That's it, Amir!" Daniel called.

"Hey, Amir!" Sophie called. "You've gone further than I did!"

But just then, Amir slipped off his board into the snow.

"Oops! He's down," said Daniel. "Let's go."

Daniel and Sophie headed down to help Amir up, but they were too slow. By the time they reached the spot where he had fallen, he was on his board again and halfway down the hill.

Sophie slid the last few metres on her knees. Daniel skidded into her and they fell in a laughing heap.

Amir walked over to them. "This is far better than *Snowboard Safari*," he said. "What are you waiting for? Let's go again!"

Henry's Visit

Zack was excited. His pen pal Henry was coming to visit, all the way from Planet Yopp. Zack and Henry kept in touch by satellite text, but today they were going to meet for the very first time.

When Henry arrived, Zack couldn't believe his eyes. It wasn't Henry's bright-green scaly skin that surprised him, but his two heads and seven wavy tentacles.

"Bopp, gloppy dopp!" said Henry cheerfully.

Zack looked at his dad. "What did he say?" he asked.

"You've forgotten to turn on your translator, silly," said Dad. He switched the control on Zack's suit to 'on'.

"Hello, Zack," said Henry.

Zack could understand him now. "Hello, Henry," he replied.

It was hard finding things to do with Henry. Zack took him roller-skating, but there weren't enough roller skates in Henry's size. They tried moon dancing, but Henry tripped everyone up.

In the end, they decided to go for a meal at Zack's favourite restaurant, the Moon Rock Café.

Henry ate more food than Zack would eat in a week. He gobbled up ten cosmic burgers, eight plates of meteor chips

and six galactic fruit salads.

"Yummy!" said Henry.

Zack wasn't so happy. He didn't have enough money left to pay for the enormous meal.

When he found out, the restaurant manager wasn't pleased. "You can do the washing up!" he said.

In the kitchen, Henry washed the dirty plates, spinning and juggling them with his tentacles. Zack could hardly believe his eyes! In just a few minutes they had finished.

The manager was amazed. "You can both have holiday jobs if you want!" he said.

Zack and Henry were thrilled. They were going to get paid and have a great holiday too.

Crazy Animals

Stomp! Stomp! Zebra's proud,
Because he stands out in a crowd.

Squeak! Squeak! Little Mouse
Scampers quickly through the house.

Roar! Roar! Hear Lion roar!
Eats his lunch and still wants more!

Miaow! Miaow! Have you seen
Naughty Kitty licking cream?

Bark! Bark! Messy Pup!
Hides his bone, then digs it up.

Baa! Baa! Clever Sheep!
Counting lambs to fall asleep.

Elephant's Trunk

Elephant loves to blow his trunk
At the start of every day.
"Tarrantarra!" he loudly trumps,
To wake his friends to play.

Elephant's trunk is useful
To shower and to squirt.
Down at the pool his friends join in,
To wash off all the dirt.

And when it comes to mealtimes,
A trunk can help once more –
To reach the highest, juiciest leaves
That jungle friends adore.

But best of all for Elephant,
When his friends are tucked up snug,
He loves to wrap his trunk around,
And give them a big hug!

Fat Cat

Eddie and Josh had set up a pet-sitting service. Their first job was to feed Fluffy, Mr and Mrs Cole's cat, while they went on holiday for a week.

"Don't forget, Fluffy needs feeding three times a day," Mrs Cole told the boys, as she handed over the huge cat.

When Mrs Cole was in the car, Mr Cole turned to Eddie and Josh. "Try not to let Fluffy eat too much!" he whispered. "See you next week."

"Mr Cole is right," said Josh a week later, as he and Eddie watched Fluffy tuck into her twenty-first bowl of food. "Fluffy definitely eats too much."

"Let's see if I can stop her," said Eddie. He made a barking noise, like a dog.

Eddie and Josh had never seen a cat move so fast. She bolted through the cat flap into the back garden and up the nearest tree.

Josh and Eddie ran outside.

"Here, Fluffy!" Josh called. But Fluffy wouldn't come down.

"Now look what you've done, Eddie!" said Josh.

"Don't panic, I'll get her down," said Eddie. He went home to fetch his toy bow and arrow and a rope. Then he tied the rope to one of the arrows and fired it over a branch.

"Hold one end of the rope, Josh," Eddie said. Slowly, Eddie pulled himself up the tree using the rope. "Phew! This is hard work!" he panted.

But just as Eddie reached the branch that Fluffy sat on, the cat scampered back down the tree trunk all by herself.

Eddie looked down. "Oh no!" he cried. "I'm stuck now!"

"It looks like we arrived home just in time!" said Mr Cole, walking into the garden. He put a stepladder against the tree and helped Eddie down. "What were you doing up there?" he asked.

Eddie and Josh explained, and Mr Cole laughed.

When Mrs Cole came outside she didn't find it quite so funny. "Fluffy doesn't usually climb trees," she said, cuddling the enormous cat and frowning at Eddie and Josh.

Fluffy purred and looked smug.

Old Roger Is Dead

Old Roger is dead and gone to his grave,
H'm ha! gone to his grave.

They planted an apple tree over his head,
H'm ha! over his head.

The apples were ripe and ready to fall,
H'm ha! ready to fall.

There came an old woman and picked them all up,
H'm ha! picked them all up.

Old Roger jumped up and gave her a knock,
H'm ha! gave her a knock.

Which made the old woman go hippity hop,
H'm ha! hippity hop!

My Funny Family

My auntie May's got a brain like a sieve –
She forgets where the things in her kitchen all live.
There are plates in the fridge and plum jam in the jug
A chop in the teapot and carrots in the mugs!

My cousin Bob's got eyes like a hawk –
He can see across the ocean from London to New York!
He says he can see unknown planets orbiting in space
And the moon has got a handlebar moustache upon its face.

My sister Sarah's got feet that love to dance –
She's danced from Perth to Benidorm, from Italy to France.
She dances in a dress trimmed with black and yellow lace,
Mum says she looks just like a bee and that it's a disgrace!

My dog Jasper's got a ferocious appetite –
To see him eating up his food is really quite a sight.
He wolfs down chips and when he's really feeling gross,
He'll polish off a cake and several rounds of buttered toast!

Pet Prize

It was school fair day. There was going to be a Best Pet Competition.

Tom's friends all brought their pets. Sammy had a hamster. Carlos had a ginger cat. Deepak had his rabbit, Sooty.

"I wish I had a pet," said Tom. Miss Bell was going to judge the competition. Her dog Chip had come too.

Chip was small and brown and had a very waggy tail.

"Can I pat him?" asked Tom.

"Yes," said Miss Bell. "He's very friendly."

Tom patted Chip. Chip wagged his tail furiously.

"I wish I had a pet like you," whispered Tom to Chip.

Chip barked understandingly.

Miss Bell looked at the pets.

She looked at a rabbit, two hamsters, four gerbils, one cat, three mice, two dogs…

"And the prize for best-groomed pet goes to… Carlos!" she said, giving him a medal.

Sammy won the prize for friendliest pet.

Deepak won the prize for most well-behaved pet.

Tom wished more and more that he had a pet of his own to enter in the competition.

Then Miss Bell looked around. "Where is Chip?" she asked. Chip was missing!

"We must find him!" said Miss Bell. She was very worried.

"I'll go and look for him," said Tom.

He looked at the book stall. Chip wasn't there.

He looked at the raffle stall. Chip wasn't there either.

Then Tom saw a wagging tail. He looked under the cake stall – and there was Chip, licking up the crumbs!

Chip wagged his tail when he saw Tom and barked.

"Time to go back," said Tom.

At the end of the competition, Miss Bell gave out a special prize.

"And this prize is for Best Pet Finder," she said with a smile. "The winner is... Tom!"

A Boy's Song

Where the pools are bright and deep,
Where the grey trout lies asleep,
Up the river and over the lea,
That's the way for Billy and me.

Where the blackbird sings the latest,
Where the hawthorn blooms the sweetest,
Where the nestlings chirp and flee,
That's the way for Billy and me.

Where the mowers mow the cleanest,
Where the hay lies thick and greenest,
There to track the homeward bee,
That's the way for Billy and me.

Where the hazel bank is steepest,
Where the shadow falls the deepest,
Where the clustering nuts fall free,
That's the way for Billy and me.

Why the boys should drive away
Little sweet maidens from the play,
Or love to banter and fight so well,
That's the thing I never could tell.

But this I know, I love to play
Through the meadow, among the hay;
Up the water and over the lea,
That's the way for Billy and me.

I'll Show You How

Oakey and Dad were walking through the woods.

"Hello!" said Squirrel. "Would you like to play?"

"All right," smiled Oakey.

"Let's climb some trees," suggested Squirrel, but Oakey wasn't sure.

"What if I fall?" he asked.

"Don't worry," Squirrel told him. "I'll show you how to do it."

And he showed Oakey what to do.

Dad nodded to Oakey. "You can try. Go ahead."

So Oakey gave it a try. "This really is fun!" he laughed.

"What's all the noise?" said a voice. Dormouse poked her head through the leaves.

"Have you come to play?"

"Um… all right," mumbled Oakey.

"Good! Let's swing from this branch," suggested Dormouse.

But Oakey wasn't sure. "What if I get it wrong?" he asked.

"Don't worry about getting it wrong," Dormouse smiled. "I'll show you how to do it." And she did.

"I'm enjoying it!" Oakey laughed.

"Well then, come and play with me," said a voice. "And you'll really have a good time."

Oakey looked down. Otter was watching from under the tree. "Follow me!" he called.

So Oakey and his friends ran after Otter to the river.

"Let's swim," said Otter.

But Oakey wasn't sure. "I've never tried it before," he said.

"I'll show you how to do it," said Otter.

Dad nodded to Oakey. "You can try. Go ahead."

"You'll have a great time, I promise!" Otter said.

And Oakey did!

"Now it's time for my game," Oakey told his friends. "Let's play leapfrog."

"Oh dear!" said Squirrel. "I've never tried this."

"Neither have I," added Dormouse. "I'm not sure."

"Me neither," agreed Otter.

"What if we're not very good?" they all said at once.

"You should always try," Oakey encouraged them. "You showed me that trying something new is fun. And besides, good friends will show you how it's done!"

Midnight Fun

Just as midnight's striking,
When everyone's asleep,
Teddies yawn and stretch and shake,
And out of warm beds creep.

They sneak out from their houses,
And gather in the dark,
Then skip along the empty streets,
Heading for the park.

And there beneath the moonlight,
They tumble down the slides,
They swoosh up high upon the swings,
And play on all the rides.

And when the sun comes peeping,
They rush home to their beds,
And snuggle down as children wake,
To cuddle with their teds!

Farm Hide-and-seek

Standing in the meadow,
Underneath the tree,
Chewing, mooing, munching,
Who can it be?

Over in the barnyard,
By the mummy sheep,
Small and white and woolly,
Who's fast asleep?

Right inside the henhouse,
Glowing in the sun,
Fluffy, bright and yellow,
Who's about to run?

Over in the paddock,
Running wild and free,
Galloping and trotting,
Who can you see?

Past the grassy meadow,
In the field beyond,
Flapping wings and quacking,
Who's in the pond?

Green Cheese

Green cheese,
Yellow laces,
Up and down
The market places.

Pit, Pat

Pit, pat, well-a-day,
Little Robin flew away;
Where can little robin be?
Gone into the cherry tree.

The Wind

Who has seen the wind? Neither I nor you;
But when the leaves hang trembling
The wind is passing through.

Who has seen the wind? Neither you nor I;
But when the trees bow down their heads
The wind is passing by.

Bagpipes

Puss came dancing out of a barn
With a pair of bagpipes under her arm;
She could sing nothing but, "Fiddle cum fee,
The mouse has married the humble-bee."
Pipe, cat! Dance, mouse!
We'll have a wedding at our good house.

Mother?

"Mother, may I go out to swim?"
"Yes, my darling daughter.
Fold your clothes up neat and trim,
But don't go near the water."

Shrovetide

Once, twice, thrice,
I give thee warning,
Please to make pancakes
Again in the morning.

Here Is the Church

Here is the church, *(link hands)*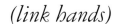

Here is the steeple, *(put index fingers together)*

Look inside, *(keeping your hands linked, turn them upside down)*

Here are the people! *(wiggle your fingers)*

Once I Was a Baby

Once I was a baby,
Now suddenly, I'm big!
And there's someone else
Sleeping in my crib.
Mum says it's my new brother,
He's very small and sweet,
With hands the size of daisies
And very smooth, pink feet.
I think I'm going to like him,
And I know that he'll like me.
Won't it be terrific
When I can hold him on my knee?

The Work of Art

Eddie had a bright idea. "Let's put a notice on the school noticeboard," he said. *"Eddie and Josh's Odd Job Service – No job too big or too small*."

"Let's do it!" said Josh.

On Thursday afternoon, Miss Price, the headteacher of the nursery next door, called the boys into her office. "I've seen your notice," she told them. "I have a job for you: I'd like you to paint the nursery playground wall."

"When shall we start?" asked Josh.

"Tomorrow after school," said Miss Price.

After school the next day, the caretaker carried some paint pots and paintbrushes into the playground.

"Miss Price didn't say what colour she wanted the wall to be painted," the caretaker said, opening the pots of paint. "I'll leave you to choose." Then he went back into his shed at the side of the playground.

Eddie and Josh looked at the paints. There was red, yellow, green and purple paint.

"We should use all the colours to paint a huge picture," said Eddie.

Josh nodded. "Let's paint some footballers," he suggested, picking up a pot of green paint.

"No, some monsters," said Eddie, taking a pot of purple paint.

"Footballers!" said Josh.

"Monsters!" argued Eddie. He flicked some purple paint at the wall.

"Footballers! " yelled Josh, flicking some green paint over Eddie's purple paint.

By the time Josh and Eddie had finished arguing, the whole wall was splattered with purple and green, and there wasn't a monster or a footballer in sight.

"Oh dear!" said Josh, staring at the wall.

They left the paints and hurried off home.

First thing on Monday morning, Josh and Eddie were called in to see Miss Price.

Miss Price was quiet for a moment. Then she clapped her hands in delight. "Well done!" she said. "What a fantastic piece of modern art!"

Eddie and Josh grinned at each other as Miss Price handed them an envelope.

"Here's your money for a job well done!" she said.

359

Lucy's Secret

"Are you coming to the school disco tonight, Lucy?" Sophie asked her classmate.

"I can't," Lucy mumbled. She pulled a book from her bag and started to read.

"I don't get it," Sophie said to Daniel after school. "Why doesn't Lucy ever want to join in anything?"

Daniel shook his head. "Maybe she's just shy. Why don't you invite her to our birthday party?"

"I can't," said Sophie. "You know Mum said we can only invite four people each, and I've already invited my four. What about you?" she asked.

"I've already invited my four people too," Daniel replied.

"We're all going ice skating, right?" Sophie said.

"Right," Daniel said with a grin. "I hope I get the hang of it quickly," he added.

The day of the party arrived. Daniel, Sophie and their friends wobbled onto the ice.

Sophie's ankles turned in and she clutched the rink wall.

Crash!

She turned towards the sound and then laughed as she saw her

brother scrambling about on the ice-covered floor. "Daniel, what are you doing down there?" she joked.

Daniel grabbed the wall and pulled himself up. His skate blades crossed and…

Crash! Down he went again.

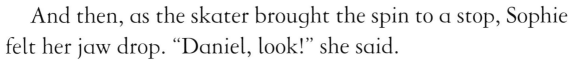

Across the ice, a skater started a slow spin. Sophie watched in awe as the girl began to twirl faster and faster until she became a blur of grey and black.

And then, as the skater brought the spin to a stop, Sophie felt her jaw drop. "Daniel, look!" she said.

Daniel turned to see where Sophie was pointing. "Is that Lucy?" he asked.

Sophie nodded.

They watched as Lucy jumped and twirled. A man stood nearby calling directions to her.

"Wow!" Daniel said. "She's great!"

The man skated away and Lucy was alone.

Sophie had an idea. She shuffled across the rink towards Lucy.

"Hi Lucy," she called.

Lucy turned round. "Oh! Hi, Sophie," she

Best Friends

Jamie and Paul were best friends. They sat next to each other in class every day. They played together and ate lunch together every day.

One day at break, Jamie pulled Paul's coat and a button flew off.

Paul and Jamie looked for the button all through break, but they couldn't find it anywhere.

Then the bell rang to say that break time was over.

"We *must* find my button," said Paul, "or my mum will be really cross!" So Jamie and Paul kept looking until they found the button.

Miss Bell told them off for being late.

"It's your fault!" Paul said to Jamie.

"It's your fault!" Jamie said to Paul.

The two friends did not talk to each other in class for the rest of the morning. They did not sit together at lunch.

The first lesson after lunch was games.

"Let's see who can change the most quickly!" Miss Bell said.

Jamie and Paul pulled out their PE bags.

"I'm going to beat Paul," Jamie thought to himself. "I'll show him!"

"I'm going to beat Jamie," Paul thought to himself. "That'll serve him right!"

The two boys raced to change into their shorts and T-shirts.

They finished at exactly the same time.

"I'm first!" cried Jamie, raising his hand. His T-shirt suddenly felt very tight under the arms.

"No, I'm first!" shouted Paul. As he raised his hand as well, he suddenly noticed that his T-shirt was almost down to his knees.

"Why are your clothes so small, Jamie?" asked Billy.

"And why are yours so big, Paul?" asked Miss Bell.

Their friends started to laugh.

"You mixed up your PE bags!" said Tilly.

Jamie and Paul laughed as well. They looked at each other.

"Friends again?" said Jamie.

"Friends again!" said Paul.

Raindrops

I love to see the raindrops
Splashing on the pavements;
I love to see the sunlight
Twinkling in the rain;
I love to see the wind-gusts
Drying up the raindrops;
I love to feel the sunshine
Coming out again!

The Dark Wood

In the dark, dark wood, there was a dark, dark house.
And in that dark, dark house there was a dark, dark room,
And in that dark, dark room, there was a dark, dark cupboard,
And in that dark, dark cupboard there was a dark, dark shelf,
And on that dark, dark shelf there was a dark, dark box,
And in that dark, dark box, there was a GHOST!

Gym Giraffe

Jeremy Giraffe loved going out with his dad to gather juicy green leaves for dinner.

"Remember – the tallest trees have the tastiest leaves, and the tiny top leaves are the tenderest!" his dad would say.

One morning Jeremy decided he wanted to gather leaves on his own, but his neck wouldn't stretch high enough. So Jeremy went back home with his neck hanging down in despair.

"Why, Jeremy, whatever is the matter?" asked his mum. When Jeremy told her, she gave his neck a nuzzle.

"You're still growing," she assured him. But Jeremy couldn't wait for his neck to grow. So he headed to the Jungle Gym to do neck lengthening exercises.

Jeremy spent the next few weeks stretching his neck with all sorts of exercises. Finally, he felt ready to reach for the highest leaves.

Next time Jeremy and his dad went out leaf gathering, Jeremy spotted some juicy leaves at the top of a very tall tree.

"I'm getting those," he said.

"They're so high up!" said Dad. But sure enough, after a big, big stretch, Jeremy reached up and ate them up!

Monkey Mayhem

Mickey, Mandy and Maxine Monkey had finished their breakfast of Mango Munch. Now they were rushing off to play.

"Be careful!" called their mum. "And DON'T make too much noise!"

"We won't!" the three mischievous monkeys promised, leaping across to the next tree. The noise echoed through the whole jungle – Mickey, Mandy and Maxine just didn't know how to be quiet!

Mickey landed on a branch. Maxine and Mandy landed beside him. Just then the branch snapped in two and they shrieked, as they went tumbling down, down, down.

The jungle shook as the three monkeys crashed to the ground, then sprang to their feet.

"Yippee!" the monkeys cheered, brushing themselves off.

The three monkeys then scrambled back up to the top of the trees. They screeched and screamed as they swung through the branches back towards home.

All through the jungle, the animals covered their ears. Nobody would ever keep these three noisy monkeys quiet!

The Double Agent

Jed was playing in an important football match at school.

"I'll come and watch!" Mum said that morning, as she left for work. But when Jed scanned the crowd of cheering parents, his mum was nowhere to be seen. Elise was there instead.

"Where's Mum?" Jed asked, when the match was over. His team had lost 3-0, and Jed was in a bad mood.

"She phoned to say she had to stay at work," Elise replied.

That evening, Mum didn't get home until after Jed's bedtime. She came in and sat down on Jed's bed. "I'm really sorry about not coming to your football match, Jed," she said. "There are problems at work. I might lose my job if things don't get better." She looked tired and worried.

Jed stopped feeling angry. Mum needs my help, he thought.

Later that night, Jed crept downstairs into the study. He clicked on Mum's inbox to see what had been happening.

The latest email in there was from Chief Officer Gridlock, Mum's boss at Unit X, the government's top spy agency.

Dear Agent
I am sorry to inform you that more government secrets have been leaked to the newspapers. You have failed in your mission to root out the double agent at Unit X. I am taking you off the case.
Gridlock

Jed sighed. Things really were bad for Mum.

The next morning, Jed didn't turn up for his paper round. Instead, he cycled to Unit X. I'm going to have a good snoop around, he thought.

Jed slipped past the security guard and up the stairs. He soon found Chief Officer Gridlock's office, but Jed could tell that Chief Officer Gridlock was already inside. There was a light shining under his door.

Jed waited around the corner. After a few minutes, Gridlock's door opened. A fierce-looking man came out and walked across the corridor to the toilet.

Jed followed. Now's my chance, he thought, as Gridlock shut the door. Jed wedged a chair under the door handle.

"Who's that?" shouted Gridlock. "Let me out!"

Jed ran back to Gridlock's office. There wasn't a moment to lose.

The computer was the best place to start looking. He needed a list of all the people who worked at Unit X. Gridlock had been checking his emails, and had left them up on his screen. Jed clicked on the 'Sent' button.

He took a deep breath. "Gridlock doesn't know much about computers!" he said. "He sends his emails to every one of his contacts – even the national newspaper editors. So he's the one who is accidentally giving away all the secrets!"

Suddenly a hand gripped Jed's shoulder. Gridlock wasn't the boss of Unit X for nothing: he had escaped from the toilet.

"Who on earth are you? I'm calling security!" Gridlock growled.

"Go on then. I'll show them what you've done!" said Jed. "I know that you are the only double agent around here. These emails prove it!"

Jed showed Gridlock what he'd found.

Gridlock sat down heavily in his chair. "I didn't mean to!" he groaned. "I've never understood computers."

"Then perhaps you should retire, and let someone take over who does," replied Jed. "And I know someone perfect for the job: Agent Frances Best."

Jed walked to the door. "If you don't tell on me, then I won't tell on you," he said. And then he hurried out.

That evening, Mum came home from work in a very happy mood. "I've had a big promotion, Jed!" she told him.

Jed gave her a hug. "Well done, Mum!" he said. Now he could look forward to some even more exciting missions.

"I couldn't have done it without you, Jed," Mum went on.

You don't know how true that is! Jed thought with a grin.

Little Tommy Tucker

Little Tommy Tucker sings for his supper.

What shall we give him?

Brown bread and butter.

How shall he cut it without a knife?

How can he marry without a wife?

A Girl Named Mag

There was a girl named Mag with feet so large

That people cried, "They're as big as a barge!"

She wished for little feet, small and round,

But when she got them, she kept falling down.

Good Night

Good night, God bless you,

Go to bed and undress you.

Good night, sweet repose,

Half the bed and all the clothes.

When Jacky's a Good Boy

When Jacky's a very good boy,

He shall have cakes and a custard;

But when he does nothing but cry,

He shall have nothing but mustard.

The Priest

The little priest of Felton,
The little priest of Felton,
He killed a mouse within his house,
And nobody there to help him.

My Shadow

I have a little shadow that goes in and out with me,
And what can be the use of him is more than I can see.
He is very, very like me from the heels up to the head;
And I see him jump before me, when I jump into my bed.

One morning, very early, before the sun was up,
I rose and found the shining dew on every buttercup;
But my lazy little shadow, like an errant sleepyhead,
Had stayed at home behind me and was fast asleep in bed.

377

The Egyptian Job

Eddie and Josh were counting all the money they had made by doing odd jobs.

"It's nowhere near enough to buy our bikes yet," Eddie said gloomily.

His mum came into the room. "I've got another odd job for you both!" she said. "I need people to hand out leaflets tomorrow." Eddie's mum ran the shop at the local museum.

The next morning, Eddie and Josh went to the museum with Eddie's mum.

She gave them a big pile of leaflets about the new Egyptian mummy exhibition.

"Give these to the people walking past," she said.

It was a freezing cold day. Eddie and Josh were soon cold and fed up.

"My fingers are like blocks of ice!" moaned Josh.

"Let's go inside," said Eddie. "We can hide in the cloakroom while we get warm again."

A cleaning trolley had been left in the washroom. On top of it were two huge rolls of toilet paper.

Eddie looked at Josh and grinned. He picked up one of the rolls and began to wrap it round and round Josh.

"This will keep you

warm!" he joked.

When Eddie had finished, Josh could hardly move.

"You look very funny!" laughed Eddie, as he gave Josh a friendly push.

Josh lost his balance and fell against the cloakroom door. The door opened and he staggered through it. "Help!" he yelled.

In front of him, a mummy display case was open. Two robbers were about to steal the priceless mummy.

"Aaargh!" screamed the robbers, seeing Josh. "That mummy has come to life!"

Josh, who was still trying to regain his balance, staggered towards them.

"Quick! Let's get out of here!" the robbers cried.

The manager hurried over to Josh and Eddie. "You've saved our prize exhibit!" he said. "You deserve a reward! I shall write you each a cheque for £100."

"Fantastic!" said Josh.

"Now we have enough money to buy those bikes we want!" said Eddie.

Little Ghost Lost

"Come along, Percy," said Mum. "It's time we took you out for your first proper spooking expedition. And what better night for spooking than Halloween!"

"Just follow us and copy what we do," said Dad. "And don't wander off on your own."

The three ghosts floated up the chimney of their home in the Haunted House, and curled out of the top like wisps of smoke.

"I don't like it out here," said Percy, timidly. "It's too dark!"

"Don't be silly," said Mum. "Ghosts aren't afraid of the dark!"

All through the evening the family of ghosts played ghostly pranks, jumping out and spooking folk, and squealing with delight as they ran away, screaming.

"I bet I could spook someone all on my own!" thought Percy.

Creeping up behind two children, he set his face in its most fearsome expression, then tapped them on their shoulders. But, as the children spun around, Percy froze in horror. He was eye to eye with two gruesome monsters!

Percy screeched and fled into the night. He didn't hear the screams behind him, or see the monsters race home, where they tore off their Halloween masks and panted out their story to their mother. Poor Percy had never heard of trick-or-treating!

Percy flitted down the streets, calling

380

for his mum and dad. Where had he left them? Finally he sank down in a doorway.

"I want my mum!" he wailed, and began to cry. Then something poked and prodded him with a sharp stick.

"What have we here then?" said a mean little voice.

"Looks like a young ghostie. Let's pinch him!" said another nasty voice. The voices belonged to two goblins.

"BOO!" said Percy, pulling a scary face. "Leave me alone!"

But the goblins just burst out laughing. It takes a lot to frighten a goblin. "Nothing scares us!" they teased.

"Oh no?" said a deep voice behind them. "How about this!"

The goblins turned to see two huge, terrifying ghosts.

"Aaaaargh!" they cried, fleeing into the night.

"Mum! Dad!" cried Percy in delight. "You found me!"

Safely back in the Haunted House, Percy said, miserably, "I'm never going to make a good spook!"

"Yes you will," soothed Mum, tucking him into bed. "After all, you certainly scared us! Next time, stick close!"

"I promise," said Percy, and in no time at all he was sound asleep, dreaming of ways to spook goblins.

Index

Index